HYENAS

A TANNER NOVEL - 45

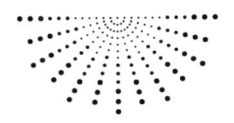

REMINGTON KANE

INTRODUCTION

HYENAS – A TANNER NOVEL – BOOK 45

Tanner accepts a challenging contract.

ACKNOWLEDGMENTS

I write for you.

—Remington Kane

1
NO HELP NEEDED

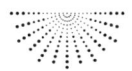

Tanner slid his finger onto the trigger of the rifle he was holding. It was just after dawn, and he was on a rooftop in Austin, Texas, and acting as backup for his protégé, Henry Knight. Henry was fulfilling a contract on three men who had run afoul of the San Antonio mob. They had done so by killing a man named Anthony. Anthony had been the son of a capo, and he'd been part of a truck heist the three men had pulled a month earlier.

One of the men had killed the capo's son during a dispute over a woman they'd both been seeing, and his friends helped him get rid of the body. After that, they went on the run, while hoping that a rival mobster would be blamed for the dead man's disappearance.

The woman who'd been involved in the love triangle gave in to feelings of guilt and confessed to a friend that she had been there when the murder occurred. That friend had been the dead man's sister. The capo put out an open contract on the three thieves and they'd been hiding ever since.

The contract was worth thirty thousand dollars. Tanner had learned about it and thought it would be a good test for Henry.

It had also been a part of his training, in developing the skill of tracking people.

They had spent three nights watching a bar in Austin where one of the men had a sister who worked as a bartender. Tanner thought the man might be foolish enough to risk seeing her. He was, arriving at closing time, and it had looked as if he'd been asking her for money, which she had given to him, along with a bottle of whiskey.

After leaving the bar, the man made a stop at a fast-food restaurant that was open all-night. Tanner and Henry then followed him back to an empty warehouse where he and his two partners were lying low.

The thieves had never had a chance to fence the goods from the truck heist and must have been desperate for money. If they attempted to use a credit card, it would have given away their location.

The cash borrowed from the bartending sister was probably all the money they had between the three of them. They would have been better off mugging someone; by visiting his sister, the thief had doomed himself and his two friends.

It was Henry's contract and would be up to Henry to fulfill. It was the first time he'd be going up against more than one target. Because of that, Tanner was ready to give assistance, but he'd decided to let Henry figure out how to go about it.

Henry had talked out loud as he considered what to do. At the time, they'd been in a car and were parked where they could keep an eye on the warehouse.

"There are three of them, so I'll have to kill them quick or one or more of them might get away; that warehouse has about six exits."

Tanner had nodded but said nothing.

"I guess I could break in there and sneak up on them, but that old, rusted metal door on the warehouse squealed loudly when the guy went back inside, and all the doors are probably like that, and the windows look like they're painted shut."

Tanner nodded again, but he remained silent.

Henry had smiled at him. "You're not going to help me, are you?"

"Would you like me to help you?"

"No. I'll think of something."

"Take your time. It looks like they're not going anywhere and will be drinking. If they get drunk, it will make your job all that much easier."

"You're right; there's no rush. I'll let them eat and drink and become sleepy, and then I'll make my move."

Tanner nodded again, and Henry laughed.

∾

As dawn approached, Henry had come up with a plan. When he told it to Tanner, he was pleased to see his mentor smile.

"I think it will work, but you'll need to be quick once you act, or one of them will hurt you."

"I'll be quick."

"And I'll get on the roof across from the warehouse to back you up. If I think you're in trouble, I'll start firing."

"You won't need to; I've got this."

"Good man," Tanner said, and left the car to head up to the roof.

Henry had given him time to settle in before he drove to the warehouse and began honking the horn. Two of the men appeared in the doorway of the warehouse. They were barefoot and wearing only their boxers and T-shirts. They looked bleary-eyed in the first rays of sunlight. Their right hands were hidden behind them and were holding guns.

Henry had his car window lowered and spoke to them. "Which one of you called for an Uber?"

The man they had followed from the bar spoke. He was bearded but was going bald on top.

"Nobody here called for a car, kid; you must have the wrong address."

Henry looked around. He wasn't searching for a number on the building, he was wondering where the third man was.

Tanner had spotted that man from his perch on the roof. The third guy had come out a different door and was hidden behind the side of the warehouse. He was in his underwear like the other two, but there was a shotgun in his hands. Tanner aimed his rifle toward him but would be ready to fire on the other two if needed.

Henry smiled at the men standing in the doorway. "I'm sorry I woke you; now you can go back to sleep." As he was saying that he brought up a silenced gun and fired two shots. He caught the bearded man in the face and his friend in the throat. He'd been so fast that they had never raised their guns.

At the same time, Henry had opened the car door. He dove to the ground and took aim at the side of the building where the third man was standing. As the guy stepped out into the open and brought the shotgun around to fire, Henry hit him in the chest with two rounds.

Up on the roof, Tanner had swiveled his rifle back to the men standing in the doorway when the shooting started, then pivoted back to the man with the shotgun. When the man who'd been hit in the throat raised a gun up, Tanner shifted that way again, only to find that Henry was shooting the man already, with a second round that finished him off.

Tanner felt tenseness in his trigger finger. Three times he'd been poised to fire, and three times found it to be unnecessary. Henry had things well-handled.

Down below, Henry was checking the bodies to make sure the men were dead. Tanner took note that he wasn't rushing about and seemed calm. The kid had what it took to be an assassin. He was fearless and in control of his emotions.

∼

Tanner made it off the roof three minutes later and found Henry parked at the curb and waiting for him. This time the nod he gave his apprentice was one of approval.

"You did great, Henry. How did you know the third man was hiding around the corner?"

"I didn't spot him at first, but then I saw the toes of his foot in my side-view mirror."

"What would you have done if you hadn't spotted him?"

"I would have apologized for waking the other two, then I would have driven off and come up with a new plan."

"Yeah. If one plan doesn't work, then try another. What you don't want to do is force a situation to fit your plan; that rarely works out well."

"I didn't think they'd be suspicious of me because of my age. They also wouldn't expect an assassin to drive up to their door and honk a horn for them."

"You were right, and it cost them, and now you have another successful contract."

"I think I'm ready to do one without you backing me up."

"I agree. The next one will be all yours. But only one guy at a time for a while. You'll also get more training."

"How soon until I can work on my own exclusively?"

"Sooner than I might have thought. Maybe next year. In the meantime, I'll try to include you in any contracts I take; that way, you'll learn faster."

"I know you don't have plans to retire anytime soon, but I can't wait to be a Tanner."

"Spenser didn't plan to retire so young, but things didn't work out that way. I'm glad I have someone to pass the Tanner name to. If anything happened to me; at least I'll know that you'll carry on the tradition."

"Nothing will happen to you."

"Sometimes fate has other ideas. But enough talk about the future, what do you plan to do with the money you earned today?"

"I'm going to buy a new motorcycle. The rest of the money will go into savings."

"We'll have to set you up in business soon, so you'll have a way to explain where your money comes from. Any ideas?"

"I could be a fashion photographer who specializes in taking photos of hot women in bikinis."

"Nice work if you can get it, but I think we'll come up with something more mundane, and that deals with cash."

"Like those food trucks you see at construction sites?"

"Yeah, or maybe a laundromat, although, they're starting to accept credit cards. It seems like cash is getting used less often everywhere, and that makes it harder to hide money."

"Things were easier when you were my age, huh?"

"They were. I didn't need a hacker and there weren't so many cameras around."

They made it to the highway and were headed home. It would be a five-hour drive. Tanner laid his head back and closed his eyes.

"I'm going to get some sleep; wake me if you get tired of driving."

"Okay, but I doubt I'll get tired. I'm pretty pumped up right now."

"It happens after a hit, especially one where you had the odds against you and came out on top. But later, you might feel like sleeping for days."

"Thanks, Cody."

Tanner opened his eyes. "For what?"

"For picking me to be Tanner Eight someday. It means a lot to me, you know. My mom was murdered when I was a boy and I felt so helpless and useless then. And when Makayla was abducted, I couldn't stop those men from taking her, and later on, they took my grandmother too. Now, I know I'll never have to feel that weak and helpless again. I'll also be able to help anyone if I need to."

"You're welcome, Henry. And I know what you mean. I

became a Tanner because of what happened to my family. I swore I'd never let anything like that happen again."

Henry sighed. "As much as I've learned from you, and as deadly as I've become, it still won't bring back my mother."

"No. Those we've lost are gone forever, but we'll never lose anyone else. And I guess that's the best we can do."

"I miss my mom, you know?"

"My mother has been dead for decades, and I still miss her; I also miss my sisters and my father. But I've got a daughter, a son, and a wife now. We can't fix the past, but we can make a future for ourselves. Sara taught me that. She made me believe I could have a life again, and not just be a Tanner. Take that lesson from me too; don't let being a Tanner become your whole life."

"I'll marry someday, I guess, but right now all I can think about is becoming good enough to be a Tanner."

"You're getting there, and you proved it today."

Tanner closed his eyes again and slid a little lower in his seat. A few minutes later he was asleep. Henry drove on with a smile lighting his face, knowing that someday he'd be a Tanner.

2

8784

Two days later, it was time for the Stark Fall Festival again.

The festival would have games, a few rides, contests, an area for children to pet and feed animals, and there would be antique cars on display. While it wasn't a car, Cody Parker, who was Tanner Seven, had decided to exhibit his fully restored 1947 Harley-Davidson Knucklehead. The red motorcycle had once belonged to Benjamin Boudreaux, who had been Tanner Three. Boudreaux had named the bike Lucille.

Cody was riding the motorcycle as he made his way to the diner for breakfast. At his side was Henry Knight. Henry's motorcycle was new but still a Harley. The former motocross racer had gone looking for speed and found it in the Harley-Davidson 114 Street Bob. The sleek bike was black and orange and its modern lines made the Knucklehead look anachronistic.

Before stopping at the diner, Cody and Henry drove past it to take in the area surrounding it. While he had no reason to suspect that anyone was laying a trap for him, Cody still surveyed the streets around the diner and looked for signs of trouble.

It was an entrenched practice with him and one that had

saved his life more than once. He had stressed the importance of vigilance to Henry and hoped to ingrain the habit of being careful into his protégé, as his mentor had done with him.

Finding nothing that raised concern, they headed back toward the diner and parked in front of it. Earlier, they had run ten miles and completed a calisthenics workout that gave them an appetite. The aromas drifting out of the diner made their mouths water with anticipation.

The diner was the only business in Stark that was open 24/7, and on this Sunday morning they were doing more business than was usual for the early hour. Like Cody and Henry, there were others having a meal before heading to the festival grounds. Some would be involved in setting things up, while others, like Cody, would be there to aid them, while also acting as security personnel.

Cody's friend, Chief of Police Steve Mendez, had talked him into becoming an auxiliary police officer again. And this year, Henry would be one as well. Extra cops were needed to keep an eye on the crowd at the festival, although no one expected there to be serious trouble.

The auxiliary officers would be given radios so they could stay in contact, and whistles in case the radios failed, and they needed to draw attention. They would also be supplied with bright yellow sweatshirts to wear. Across the front and back of each shirt in bold black lettering were the words: Auxiliary Police.

Cody and Henry would take the radios and the whistles but had passed on the yellow sweatshirts. Instead, Mendez had given them deputy badges to wear. Cody's badge had the number seven on it, and Henry's bore the number eight. They wore them pinned to their belts. Cody and Henry were dressed alike in jeans, boots, and long-sleeved chamois shirts. Henry's shirt was blue while Cody's was black. Henry was also bearded.

The auxiliary cops were teamed up with the regular deputies

and given an area of the festival to patrol. Cody would be teamed up with the Deputy Chief of Police, Clay Milton. Clay had helped to defend the Parker Ranch from an attack by Ordnance Inc. and Cody had gotten to know him since coming back to town. He liked Clay, and Milton had been invited to the ranch more than once, along with his English girlfriend, Amelia Harper.

Henry would spend the day at Chief Mendez's side. He was looking forward to it. The chief was a friend, and along with Cody he had helped Henry to restore an old car.

∽

THE STARK DINER HAD BEEN AROUND FOR DECADES. IT HAD A large seating area in the middle that held over a dozen tables while there were booths along the left side and the back. The counter was on the right, near the entrance, and had a line of red stools. Although old, the building was in good shape and the booths and stools had been reupholstered recently. As a teen, Cody had spent a lot of time in the diner, that is, after he'd gotten his chores on the ranch done.

Cody returned the smile of the waitress as he entered the diner, then waved a greeting to several people he knew. Henry did the same, including sending a wave to the table where the mayor was seated. The greeting wasn't intended for the mayor, Jimmy Kyle, but went to his niece, fourteen-year-old Chrissy Kyle. The redheaded girl had a crush on Henry and had waved to him first. When Jimmy and his brother, Kent, had seen who Chrissy was waving to, they sent frowns along.

Cody ignored them and he and Henry settled in a booth toward the back. From where Cody sat, he could see the entrance, while Henry had a view of the corridor that led to a rear door. If anyone entered the diner, they would know about it. They were ever vigilant and needed to be, particularly Cody. It was unlikely that an enemy would track him down to Stark,

Texas, but unlikely didn't mean impossible. If that happened, he wouldn't easily be taken unawares.

Not that he had a lot of enemies who were still above ground. Going up against Tanner was a great way to ensure that one never reached old age. However, there were exceptions, such as a young mobster named Liam Murphy. Liam had gone into hiding years earlier, but Tanner hadn't forgotten him. Wherever Liam was hiding, he would be wise to stay there. If he came after Tanner again, he would not survive the encounter.

There were also those who would kill Tanner for the boost it would give their reputations. By killing Tanner, their status in the criminal world would rise exponentially. Hundreds had died while trying to kill the man, and if anyone accomplished the act they would be catapulted to fame in certain circles.

The food arrived at the table before Cody and Henry had finished their first cups of coffee. As they sipped on the brew, they had been entertained by a conversation going on at the counter. There were two old men seated there. Their names were Garrett Smith and Howard Jones.

The two could be found in the diner most days. Garrett was an atheist and a democrat while Howard was a devout Catholic and a republican. They argued over everything but had been best friends since childhood. Residents of Stark got a kick out of the bickering pair, as their conversations were often comical.

Cody knew they were very old, because they had seemed old when he'd left the town as a boy of sixteen, more than twenty-five years ago. They argued about something every day, with the topics ranging from politics to poltergeists. Today's argument was about religion.

Garrett, a retired teacher, wore his white hair long and favored jeans, sweatshirts, and sneakers. Howard, a former accountant, was bald, and still wore a suit and tie every day along with a pair of sturdy shoes.

The sweatshirt Garrett had on today was bright green and

had bold numbers printed on it in black. They were the numbers 4716.

From what Cody had gathered, Garrett had joined an online group of atheists with thousands of members. Each member had claimed an hour of the year and declared it as the time of Jesus Christ's return to earth. They hadn't been converted, rather, it was an attempt to prove the bible false.

In the book of Matthew, it is stated that no man will know the day and hour of Jesus' return. By claiming an hour and asserting that it would be the time Jesus returned, the atheists, who called themselves the 8784s, believed they had thwarted that prophecy.

The name of the group came from the number of hours in a year, if you included leap year—24 hours times 366 days equaled 8,784. With Garrett claiming the number 4716, he had been given the hour between noon and one p.m. on July 16th or 17th. The exact day would depend on whether it was a leap year. Howard proclaimed the idea behind the 8784-group blasphemy and called Garrett a fool.

"You don't believe in Jesus, so how can you claim to know the hour and day of his return?"

Garrett grinned a devilish smile as he answered. "I don't believe in him today, but you can bet your ass I'll believe in him in July when my hour rolls around. I'll proclaim to anyone who will listen that the 'Lord' is coming back at that day and hour. The same is true for all the others in my group. So you see, either someone will know the day and hour, or it will all be bunk. There's no middle ground, Howard, and that will prove the bible is wrong."

"No, it won't," said a small voice.

Everyone looked over at the mayor's table. It had been young Chrissy Kyle who had spoken, but with all eyes on her, she blushed and lowered her head.

"What's that you said there, little girl?" Howard asked.

Chrissy raised her chin. She looked annoyed by Howard's use of the term, "Little girl."

"She didn't say anything," Kent Kyle said, as he gave his daughter a disapproving look.

"She did say something," Garrett said. "She said that I was wrong."

Howard laughed "Of course, you're wrong. You haven't been right about anything since I've known you."

"I can't be wrong. We have every hour of every day covered. That means that someone will know the day and hour of Jesus' so-called 'return,' which proves the bible is a bunch of hooey."

Chrissy asked a question. "What if he came back during the hour you picked?"

"What if he did?" Garrett said. "That would make me the man who knew the hour and the day of his return."

A small smile appeared on Chrissy's lips before she spoke again. "What if you died two seconds before that hour started? Then there would be no one who would know the day and hour, right?"

Garrett looked puzzled for a moment, then his mouth fell open as he realized that Chrissy was right. If he or any of his fellow atheists in the 8784-group died prior to their hour's arrival, there would be no one who "knew" the day and hour.

Howard slapped a knee and laughed at his friend. "The little girl is right. And anyway, you would never have really believed in the Lord's return; you'd have only been pretending to do so."

Garrett looked dejected, but he decided to cheer himself up by ordering a piece of cherry pie. Before the pie came, he and Howard were arguing about a new topic—UFOs. Howard insisted there was no such thing as aliens, while Garrett began reciting credible stories about UFOs that had come from reliable sources.

Henry was smiling at Chrissy. "She's a smart girl."

"Does she still follow you around sometimes?" Cody asked.

"Yeah, but I don't mind."

"She's cute."

"And a kid."

"But she won't always be one."

"Yeah, but that's years from now."

Cody nodded. When he looked over at Chrissy Kyle, he saw that she was staring at Henry with a dreamy expression.

~

CODY'S FAMILY ARRIVED AT THE FESTIVAL AROUND TEN A.M.

Along with Sara, Lucas, and Marian, was their live-in housekeeper, Franny Facini.

Henry's grandmother, Laura, had come along, as had Cody's neighbors, Caroline Lang; her young son, Jarod; and her father, Raymond "Crash" Wyman. Caroline's little sister, Olivia, was also present, as she was home from college. Olivia was going to school at UCLA.

Henry and Olivia had once been a couple and remained friends. Olivia had a new boyfriend in California, while Henry dated infrequently. Instead, he kept busy with his college courses and his training to follow in Cody's footsteps as a Tanner.

Cody was enjoying his time at the festival although he had to work. He and Clay had broken up a fight between two teenagers, but other than that it was quiet. That was good. At an earlier festival, gunfire had broken out between two groups of thieves.

Cody faced enough danger while he acted as Tanner. At home in his quiet town, he wanted peace. This year's festival went well, and everyone enjoyed themselves.

Since they had arrived early to help set up things, Cody and Henry left the festival as the crowd was thinning. Cody arrived back home with his family and had to carry a sleeping Lucas inside. The boy had been playing games with other children and exhausted himself. Marian was also asleep and was in her mother's arms.

Dinner was delayed until the children woke from their naps, and they were put to bed later than usual after the family watched a movie together.

Once they were in their own bed, Cody and Sara made love before falling asleep. As he was closing his eyes, Cody smiled, having enjoyed the day. He was at home on his own ranch and had his family around him.

Life was good.

3

COMPANY ON THE WAY

The following morning, Cody was in the passenger seat of a helicopter being piloted by Henry.

The young man had already flown the required hours to get his license and was now using flight time to gain experience. Cody came along and had been hoping to fly as well, but there had been a minor mechanical problem with the other helicopter they were renting. The flaw was discovered during the preflight check. Since Henry needed the flight time more than Cody, it was decided that Henry would fly the remaining helicopter.

They were in the air for over an hour before returning to the airport. Henry landed the craft smoothly and told Cody that he couldn't wait to fly again.

"I'd love to own one someday."

"They don't come cheap," Cody said.

"Yeah, but I'll be making good money in the future. Hey, why don't you buy one? You have the money."

"And once I bought it, then you could borrow it?"

Henry grinned. "Exactly."

Henry had afternoon classes to attend at his college and Cody returned to the ranch. Before heading to the house, he spoke with his ranch foreman, Rick Winhoffer, and checked in with Casey Rocco, the man who ran the Parker Training Center for him.

Things on the ranch were running smoothly, although there was a minor issue with personnel after two of the hands quit unexpectedly. Winhoffer assured Cody that he should have no problem finding replacements.

"You pay better than most ranches, Cody. And I've already got four men coming in for interviews tomorrow. In the meantime, Bobby has been lending me a hand. That kid is a hard worker."

Bobby was Bobby Lincoln, the young caretaker for the ranch. He could be annoying at times because he loved to ask questions about every little thing, but Cody agreed with Winhoffer's assessment of Bobby. After doing his own work, Bobby was always willing to pitch in where needed.

"Keep track of his hours for me, Rick, and I'll pay him at double the usual rate."

Winhoffer laughed. "You should; he works twice as hard as most men. That is, when he's not asking questions."

"He does like to talk, but he never asks the same questions twice. I think someday he'll know this ranch as well as we do."

"I bet he will," Winhoffer said.

~

Casey Rocco was busy teaching a firearms class when Cody arrived at the Parker Training Center. Casey was forty and had put twenty years into a military career. Casey had successfully completed both Ranger School and the Special Forces Qualification Course. He was an ideal pick to oversee the staff that would teach the skills the Parker Training Center offered.

The center had two courses available. There was elite armed

guard training, and a program designed to ready military recruits for the rigors of basic training. The center had an obstacle course modeled after the Special Forces course nicknamed Nasty Nick. There was a large shooting range, and a gym that took up over four thousand square feet.

Cody had given Casey Rocco an equal say in who they hired for the staff, and Casey had recommended several of his former military buddies. Cody was happy with the staff, which currently consisted of nineteen people. They had started with sixteen, but the staff had grown along with the business, and business was good.

The Parker Training Center was a full-time facility. It provided sleeping quarters and meals to all who attended. Those who would be trained as elite armed security officers signed up for an intense eight-week course, while the basic training course was nine weeks. Individuals could sign up and pay their own way, but the facility was targeting organizations to be their main customers. This was particularly true for the security sector.

Early on, one company, a start-up itself, had signed a contract for the Parker Training Center to train forty of its personnel. The president of that company was a friend of Casey Rocco's. Casey's connections alone would have made him an excellent choice to lead the center. Since then, they had trained over a thousand men and women and the list of clients had expanded.

Casey was six-foot-three and had dark hair and brown eyes. He was married with one child, a girl. He and his wife had been looking to settle down. Settling down was difficult in the military, where you could be transferred to a different location with little notice, which was why Casey retired from the service. Cody liked the man and Sara got along well with his wife, Deidre.

Casey finished the class and greeted his boss with a smile while delivering good news.

"I was going to call you. I just got a text telling me that we got the contract with GuardTech."

Cody smiled back at Casey. "That's for over two hundred guards, right?"

"Two hundred and twelve over a six-month period, and there will be more in the future if they renew the contract."

Cody offered his hand. "Great work, Casey. And it looks like we'll need more people."

"Just one more. Someone with firearms experience. That way, I can dedicate all my time to managing things around here."

"Let me know when you find someone."

"I will."

∽

Cody returned home to discover that Franny was looking after the children while Sara was in the room they used as a home office.

After kissing him hello, Sara asked Cody a question. "How would you feel about me going back to work again?"

"As a private investigator?"

"I would be one, yes, but I was thinking of working as a bounty hunter."

"That might mean you'd have to be away from home at times."

"Yes."

Cody shrugged. "I guess it would work with Franny here. I do think we should try to avoid us both being away at the same time too often."

"So, you think it's a good idea?"

"I think you should do what you want as much as you can. Lucas is no longer a baby, and although Marian is young, she's not an infant. And Franny is like family and will look out for them. I do have a suggestion though."

"What's that?"

"Blue Steele is the best there is at tracking down people and she worked as a bounty hunter for years. Why not give her a call and ask for her advice."

"That's a great idea. And she lives right here in Texas, right?"

"She and her husband own a small ranch outside Fort Worth. That's about five-hundred miles away."

"I've only met her once. Maybe you should call her and ask if she'd be willing to give me some advice."

Cody took out his phone. "I'll call her right now."

"Now?"

"Why not?"

After three rings, Cody heard a female voice answer. There was a decided Texas accent detectable, even though Blue only spoke a few words.

"Hello, Tanner. I was just talking about you."

"To who?"

"To Thomas. He and Rhona are here."

"Lawson is there? Does that mean he needs Predator?"

Predator was the name of the group Thomas Lawson had formed to handle difficult and dangerous people or situations. Tanner was part of a team that included Blue Steele, his cousin, Mr. White, and Jake Caliber.

"It's not about Predator. He was in the area, and I invited him to dinner. Why are you calling? It's not like you to be chatty."

"I'm calling for Sara. She's thinking of becoming a bounty hunter and wanted some advice from the best, and that means you."

"I'll help if I can. Give me her number and I'll call her."

"Thanks Blue," Tanner said, and then he recited Sara's phone number.

"Got it," Blue said. "Now hold on, Thomas wants to speak to you."

The phone was passed, and Lawson came on the line.

"Hello Tanner, I was going to call you soon. I have work for you if you want it."

"I'll help anytime you need me, Thomas; you know that. If it weren't for you, I wouldn't have been able to reclaim my name and land. I assume it's a contract?"

"Actually, there are two of them. I'll let you have your pick and take a recommendation from you on who to approach with the remaining one."

"Two contracts? And they're both difficult?"

"Oh yes. If it's possible, I'd like to meet with you to discuss them."

"Today?"

"Tomorrow would be better, say around seven p.m.? I have other concerns to see to in Dallas. Maybe Rhona and I can come for dinner. I really did enjoy Franny's cooking."

Cody smiled. "You're not alone there. What would you like Franny to make?"

"I'm sure anything will be good... but I did quite relish that lasagna she made last time."

"I'll put in a request, and I look forward to seeing you and Rhona. If there's nothing else, say goodbye to Blue for me."

"I will. And I'll see you tomorrow evening."

Sara smiled as Cody put away his phone. "Thomas is coming for dinner tomorrow?"

"Yeah, and he's got a contract for me. Two contracts, and I'll get to pick the one I want."

"Knowing you, you'll pick the hardest one."

"I will, but they'll both be difficult, or Thomas wouldn't be involved."

Footsteps could be heard approaching the doorway and Franny appeared holding Lucas's hand.

"Marian is down for her nap, but this young man is still full of energy."

When Lucas saw his father, he ran over to him. "Hi, Daddy. Can we go for a ride?"

Cody picked up his son. "We can do that." He then let Franny know that they would be having guests the next day, and that Lawson would be pleased if she made lasagna.

"I'll make extra so Mr. Lawson can take some with him when he leaves. He ate two servings the last time he was here."

Sara's phone rang. When she answered it, she found it was Blue calling her. Cody left her to talk in private and headed to the stables with Lucas, while Franny went off toward the kitchen. As Cody grabbed his saddle in preparation to ride, he wondered about the contracts Lawson mentioned and hoped that at least one of them would prove to be interesting. He was pulled from his musing as Lucas tugged on his sleeve.

"What's up, buddy?"

"Can I ride alone?"

"You mean your pony?"

"Uh-huh."

"Okay."

Cody placed a saddle on a white pony, then helped Lucas to climb up onto the animal. Although his son was too young to ride alone, he could sit in the saddle while Cody walked in front of him and guided the pony along with a lead rein. In another year or so, the boy would be able to handle the pony by himself. Cody looked forward to the day when he and Lucas could ride across their land together side-by-side. Soon after, they would be joined by Marian.

As he guided Lucas along on the pony, Cody's thoughts returned to the contracts Lawson had. While he loved being home, he still looked forward to working. Somewhere out there were two targets worthy of death. Once he chose one, they were as good as dead.

4

CHOOSE WHO DIES

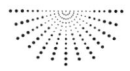

SARA'S CONVERSATION WITH BLUE STEELE TURNED INTO AN invitation. Blue told Sara that she would take her along on a bounty hunt when they both had the time to devote to it, which would probably be after the holidays were over. Sara thanked her and was looking forward to it.

Henry was invited to dinner. Cody wanted him to sit in on his meeting with Lawson and Rhona O'Donnell. As his apprentice, Henry had sat in on such meetings before. Cody knew that in the years to come, when he was no longer acting as Tanner, and when Lawson was retired, it would be Rhona offering contracts to Henry.

Tanner wondered if Henry, as Tanner Eight, might not be one of the few elite assassins left at that time. Given the growing prevalence of omnipresent cameras and other surveillance systems, it might become impossible to operate as an assassin without someone in power behind the scenes running interference for you.

Anyone without such assistance would be identified through facial recognition software and their movements tracked and recorded. Add in thermal sensors and a sophisticated smart grid and fading away after a hit might be impossible.

When he thought more deeply about the coming advances in technology, Cody wondered if a Tanner would even be necessary in the emerging world of AI and advanced high tech. Why send a man or a woman to kill a target when you could send a micro attack drone half the size of a fly to do the same job? In fact, why have people do anything at all? If robots were fashioned to perform any task, be it assassination; construction; surgery; the composing and playing of music, why would there be the need for humans as anything other than consumers? The robots could even be created that would perform the designing, manufacture, and repair of themselves. If that came about, what necessity would there be for work of any kind?

While many saw work as a curse, Cody did not. Work, particularly work of ones own choosing, gave you purpose and the opportunity to excel and expand your skills. When no one needed to work, and life was all about play, it seemed inevitable that boredom would be the result.

Striving to be the best assassin who ever lived had given his life purpose and made him stretch himself to the limits of his abilities, and then go beyond them. The same would have been true had his goal been to be a master violinist, architect, or a physician. It took work, immense amounts of work, and dedication to be the best, and such effort molded you and made you better. In contrast, a life of endless leisure would breed weakness and a malaise of the spirit. If such a world ever emerged, Cody hoped he wouldn't live long enough to see it.

For now, there was still the need for elite assassins, and there were none better than Tanner.

~

LAWSON ARRIVED IN A LIMO AND HAD A CARLOAD OF MEN ALONG as security. Tanner recognized the men and they had been to the ranch before. They would be dining as well but would be in the kitchen while Lawson and Rhona supped in the dining room.

There were two exceptions. One was Damon Stark. He was Lawson's go-to man and in charge of his security detail. The other man was Lawson's limo driver, Billy Ortiz. Lawson considered both men his friends, and Cody had come to know them, and liked both.

Damon had helped Cody during the aftermath of his destruction of Ordnance Inc. The young black man was trusted by Lawson and had also aided Cody's cousin, Mr. White, on more than one occasion. Billy Ortiz had a connection to White as well, as he had been an acquaintance of Cody's cousin for years.

The two men dined with Lawson, Rhona, and Cody's family, and there was no conversation concerning the reason for Lawson's visit during the meal. That would be discussed in private.

~

LAWSON AGAIN HAD TWO SERVINGS OF FRANNY'S LASAGNA. AND HE beamed with delight when she presented him with a container of the food to take with him. She had packed it in a foam cooler lined with ice packs.

"Now that will keep for about eight hours, but after that you'll need to refrigerate it," Franny told him.

Rhona laughed. "It may not last that long. Thomas will probably eat it while we're on the plane."

"I just might," Lawson said, and he thanked Franny for her kindness.

Henry, and Damon Stark found they had a mutual interest in motocross, as Stark had been a racer as a teen. Billy was also in on the conversation, as he had ridden motorcycles in his younger years, and had a love of all motor sports.

It was a pleasant meal spent with friends, but Cody was anxious to learn about the contracts Lawson had. After dessert had been enjoyed, Cody suggested that Lawson, Henry, and

Rhona join him in the office. Once they were inside and settled comfortably, Rhona opened her laptop to get to work.

∽

RHONA USED AN ADAPTER TO LINKUP HER LAPTOP WITH THE office's flat screen TV. After she pushed several keys, the faces of two men appeared on the television screen. They looked to be in their late-twenties or early-thirties.

That the men were related was obvious. Their features were similar, and they had the same dark-blond hair and gray eyes. The eyes of the man on the right, while revealing intelligence, didn't have the gleam of brilliance that was displayed in the other man's eyes. There was also something about him that spoke of brutishness and cruelty. Tanner had spent much time around such people and knew the type by sight.

Lawson pointed toward the screen. "You're looking at Kirk and Niko Hyena, Tanner. They're brothers, and Kirk is the oldest by two years. He's the man on the left."

"Their last name is Hyena, like the animal?" Henry asked.

"It is," Rhona said. "It's one of the rarest surnames, and they were born in Finland before their parents moved to Africa."

"What have they done that makes them eligible to be my targets?" Tanner asked. And yes, although he was at home on his ranch, he was Tanner now. With the prospect of a new contract, Cody had become all business, and his intense eyes shone with interest.

"First, we'll give you their background," Lawson said, then he nodded at Rhona.

Rhona stood and walked over to stand beside the TV. "Kirk and Niko Hyena were orphaned when Kirk was four and Niko was a month shy of turning two. They were later adopted by a dictator named Tristan Nilsson and his wife. Nilsson ruled a small country in Africa named Almalia. Eight years ago, Kirk and Niko murdered Nilsson, his wife, and the other two children the Nilssons had adopted; they were fraternal twins, a boy and a girl, and they were only eleven years old. In other words, they murdered their own family. This was done so they could take over control of the country. Once they had done so, they stopped using the name Nilsson and started using their original surname again."

"They're in Africa?" Tanner asked.

"No," Rhona said. "They lost control of their nation three weeks ago and barely survived. Right now, they're in Mexico. Their ouster left the country in a civil war. Kirk and Niko's supporters are battling the group that's taken over. That group wants to institute a democratic republic, while the Hyenas' supporters want the Hyenas' dictatorship reestablished."

"Why would anyone want someone to rule over them?" Henry asked.

"Because they were profiting from the arrangement," Tanner said.

Rhona nodded. "That's correct. The Hyenas had carried on what the dictator, Nilsson, had created, a system that enriched themselves and those that did their bidding, while the rest of the country was forced to slave away for the crumbs that were left behind. Like their adoptive father, they made millions in the drug trade, as well as in human trafficking. They also took control of their father's fortune. This included tens of millions gained by pillaging the nation's diamond mine. Until recently, it appeared that the Hyenas' supporters would be defeated, but that's changed. The Hyenas' followers have gained an edge by procuring new weapons."

Tanner looked at Lawson. "I'm guessing that the other side will be getting new weapons as well, yeah?"

Lawson smiled. "That would be a good guess, although, officially, the United States isn't involved in the region. Unofficially, the rebels will be given what they need to win and defeat the Hyenas' allies. And in any event, it's been decided that the Hyenas need to be put down. That's where you come in."

"Why do I have to choose between them? Why not let me kill both of them?"

"They're not in the same location, although they are close to each other. Kirk is being guarded by a small army of men inside an estate that's on the border of the Chihuahuan Desert in Mexico. Niko is at a separate location deeper in the desert that's about thirty miles away. An informant told us that it was Kirk's idea they separate. That way, if one of them was killed, the other could flee and go into hiding elsewhere."

"That tells me he's aware that he and his brother are at risk from an assassin despite the precautions they've taken. He sounds like a man who won't do anything foolish, like stand in front of an open window."

"Kirk Hyena is intelligent, and he has faith that his people will win the fight and that he'll be able to return to his adoptive country to rule again. If he can't make it, then his brother, Niko, will do so."

"Thirty miles isn't very far. I could kill one and then kill the other, and I could do it within an hour if I could get my hands on a plane or a helicopter."

Lawson nodded. "That might work, but it would be a great risk. In the time it would take you to reach the surviving brother, they could escape and go into hiding. We need both these men to die within minutes of each other."

"How would one brother know if the other is dead? Even if they keep in contact every hour, that will still allow me time to reach the surviving brother."

"Kirk Hyena wears a device that registers his heartbeat, as does Niko Hyena. If either man dies, the devices will send out an alert to the surviving brother using a satellite link. They'll each know within seconds if the other is dead. And knowing that, they'll flee. This is why we need you and whoever else is involved to assassinate the brothers simultaneously, or as close to that as you can get."

"And I get to pick which one I want to go after?"

"Yes," Rhona said, then she smiled at Henry. "Perhaps your apprentice could handle the other man."

Henry smiled back at her. "I'd like the chance, but if these targets are tough enough that you came to Tanner, I'm not at that level yet."

"Romeo is," Tanner said. "Or perhaps the assassin named Taran. But what makes these men so hard to kill?"

Rhona retook her seat and brought up a different image on the screen. It showed an aerial view of a large home located in a desert region. The house had several other structures near it, and it was all surrounded by a wall. Tanner recognized it for what it was, a fortress.

"This is where Kirk Hyena is living. We're told that wall is fifteen feet high and that there are electronic sensors embedded in it. If anyone approaches it who isn't wearing a device that sends out a recognized signal, a warning siren sounds off. There are also men guarding it, scores of cameras, and the home's security force numbers more than fifty."

"That's a lot of men," Tanner said. "Who are they?"

"They're cartel soldiers. The Hyenas have friends in the drug trade. They'll repay those friends once they regain control of their country. That can't happen."

"And what about Niko? Is he in a similar fortress?"

Rhona brought up a new image on the screen and placed it beside the photo of the fortress. It displayed a desert region that had several rock formations and a hillier terrain, but there were no structures visible.

"What are we looking at here?" Tanner asked.

"That's Niko Hyena's hideout. The entire thing is underground somewhere in that vicinity. It was built by a cartel leader as a doomsday shelter. We know little about it, but it's rumored to have land mines that can be activated remotely."

Tanner left his seat and moved closer to the TV. He then leaned in and stared at the photo displaying the land where the doomsday shelter was located. "What details can you tell me about this underground fortress?"

"We don't have any. We assume Niko can observe much through cameras hidden near the bunker's entrances. There are said to be numerous tunnels leading to the surface, including some that go on for miles, but that's conjecture. The cartel leader who had the shelter built ordered the crew that constructed it to be slaughtered afterwards, including the man who designed it. He was paranoid and suspicious of others."

"Someone must know details about the place."

"Maybe, but if so, we've yet to come across them. The cartel leader designed the shelter to be self-sufficient. From all accounts, the man was distrustful of everyone. He wouldn't even risk having a bodyguard nearby."

"You talk about him in the past tense. What happened to him?"

Rhona smirked. "Ironically, he died of suicide."

Tanner was staring at the screen. The underground shelter seemed a worthy challenge. On the other hand, getting to a target that was surrounded by fifty armed men would also be an enticing test of his skills and ingenuity.

He looked at Lawson. "Do you need me to choose a target right now?"

"Not at all. The Hyena brothers will stay where they are until they receive word from their forces that it's safe to return to Africa. It could be weeks or even months before the battle going on there ends."

"Before I choose, I'd like to know as much about each man as I can. Let me have everything you know about them."

Rhona reached into an outer compartment on her laptop bag and removed a file folder. "There's not much here I'm afraid, and it's mostly from one source."

"Who is the source?"

"When the Hyenas fled Africa, they took along several of their servants. One of them was an older English woman named

Jane Crowley; Mrs. Crowley had been their nanny when they were boys."

"Their nanny? That sounds like she would know them very well."

"She does, but she was shocked and appalled when they slaughtered their parents and siblings. She was wise enough not to reveal her true feelings and stayed loyal to them. Once they were in Mexico, she and several others managed to slip away and made it into the United States."

"She made contact with the authorities here?"

"No. She was picked up by the U.S. Department of Immigration. When it became clear who she was, she was offered a deal to be allowed to stay in the country. She answered every question put to her about the Hyenas and was granted a green card and given permanent resident status."

"You said she was English. Why wouldn't she have wanted to return home instead?"

"Her only surviving relative, a sister, lives in Vermont. Mrs. Crowley went to live with her."

"I'll also need everything you have on these fortresses the Hyenas are using."

Rhona pointed to the file folder. "It's all in there."

Tanner held up the thin file. "You said there wasn't much, but I didn't think you meant this little."

"I know, and I wish there was more, but as you can imagine, it's not easy gaining intelligence on criminal assets inside another country, particularly that underground bunker being used by Niko Hyena."

Tanner turned his attention back to Lawson. "I'll need time to decide which target to go after, and I might do research of my own on both targets. If I'm going to hand one of these contracts over to a friend to fulfill, I want to give them every advantage I can."

Lawson smiled. "That's fine. Take all the time you need to come to a decision. And once you've chosen which target you'll go after, I'll also take your recommendation about who to use concerning the remaining man. Additionally, if needed, a joint task force of American and Mexican federal agents could be formed. Given how many escape tunnels the bunker is rumored to have, it might be best to have dozens of people at that site instead of one man." Lawson grinned. "Unless, of course, that man is you."

Tanner nodded while staring at the two images shown on the screen. If he could somehow split himself in two, he'd love to go after both targets.

After sighing. He told Lawson that he would have his decision within a week or two.

5

DECISIONS, DECISIONS

Cody stayed up late to go over the reports he'd been provided.

The information on the fortress and the bunker was almost useless given its generalness. There was little knowledge gained from reading it that couldn't have been gathered by staring at the aerial photographs that had been taken of them. The underground hideaway sheltering Niko Hyena was almost a complete mystery concerning its details. And yet, Tanner had to agree that the supposition about there being land mines and hidden tunnels made sense.

The interview of the Hyenas' former servant, Jane Crowley, was more informative. She had known the men since they were boys and could provide a psychological profile of each of them.

Tanner was impressed by whoever it was that had questioned the woman. They had asked exhaustive queries and on a variety of topics. It seemed certain they had learned everything Jane Crowley knew about Kirk and Niko Hyena.

At the end of the interview, they had elicited Crowley's opinion about the men. She offered it and revealed a new layer about her former employers' personalities.

"I think they are both monsters in human form... but I can't say that I blame them fully for what they've become. Tristan Nilsson was a monster himself, and he raised those boys to be like he was. He didn't consider it to be a problem when they abused others, and I'm sure he never imagined that they would someday turn against him. Doing so was Kirk's idea, I'm sure of that. He's as cold a man as you could ever meet. As for Niko, he loves his brother, and he would do anything Kirk asked of him."

The interviewer remarked that Jane Crowley began crying before she spoke again. And when she did speak, it was in a croaking voice.

"Tristan Nilsson was a dictator, and his wife, Hannah, was a harpy. But those children... Kirk should have spared his younger brother and sister. I'll never forgive him for murdering the twins, and I pray that someday he'll be punished for it."

Kirk Hyena was twenty-nine. He had a thin build, a genius IQ, and was an ardent collector of rare stamps. He was also a pilot and had owned three planes back in Almalia. He'd had one serious relationship while going to college in France. That relationship ended when the young woman refused to agree to live with Kirk in his country. Since that time, he'd satisfied his sexual desires with prostitutes.

Niko Hyena was twenty-seven. While he was not a dolt, neither was he brilliant. He had a muscular body and enjoyed using it while engaged in extreme activities such as skydiving, high-altitude skiing, and big game hunting. He was also into scuba diving and had participated in three triathlons.

Concerning the big game hunting, Jane Crowley had stated that it was rumored among the servants that Niko had also hunted men for sport.

Tanner had been surprised when he came across a remark that indicated Niko was aware of him. Years earlier, Niko had asked his father for permission to travel to the United States. He had been keen to collect a two-million-dollar bounty that had been placed on the head of someone. That someone had been Tanner. Niko wasn't allowed to leave the country, but he had stated that he would have claimed the bounty if he'd been in on the hunt for Tanner.

Niko had a connection to Maurice Scallato as well, as did Kirk. Their adoptive father, Tristan Nilsson had hired the assassin more than once and had known Scallato personally. Niko had been a fan of Scallato. He couldn't have been pleased when the news reached him that Tanner had killed the man.

While Kirk was the calm, cool, and collected type, Niko had an abrasive personality and was a hothead who often got into fights. Tanner thought that Kirk had been wise to place his brother inside the underground bunker instead of letting him have the fortress. If Niko had annoyed or angered his guards, they might have been tempted to kill the man themselves. And if the fortress came under attack, Niko might have joined in the defense instead of seeking shelter or fleeing.

If the bunker defenses were automated as assumed. Niko wouldn't have an opportunity to fight, because the defense systems would handle his problems for him.

Tanner was intrigued by the bunker. The fact that so little was known about it made it an attractive target. On the other hand, overcoming the odds at the fortress was appealing. Cody decided to sleep on it and let his subconscious mull over the choice presented to him. He fell asleep while recalling strategies contained in the Book of Tanner that might help him to kill his target, whoever that target turned out to be.

~

HENRY CAME BY THE NEXT MORNING AND ASKED IF HE COULD look over the file concerning the contracts. Cody gave it to him and had him read it inside the office. When he returned to the office after getting in a workout in his home gym, Henry had read the entire thing.

"Do you have any comments or suggestions?"

"I think they're both tough, but if I had to choose, I might go after the guy in the underground bunker. I'm wondering if there might not be a way to hack into whatever computer is controlling the defenses."

"Hmm, that's a good idea. I hadn't thought of that. I think I'll give Tim Jackson a call and ask him to see if he can access the site's computer."

Henry grinned. "I'm glad I could help. I can also help you when you move in to complete the contract."

"Don't you have classes?"

"Yeah, but I'll be on winter break soon. If you make your move then, I'll be free to give you a hand."

"I should be ready about that time. I want to have this done before the new year arrives."

Cody flipped through the file until he came to the photos that displayed the aerial views of the two sites. After considering something, he asked Henry what his schedule was like.

"I've got two classes later today and one tomorrow morning. After that, I'm free the rest of the week."

"How'd you like to take a trip to Mexico?"

Henry looked surprised by the question. "What? You've decided which Hyena to go after?"

"Not yet. But I want to get a look at both sites before I decide. I can only do that by visiting the area."

"I'm ready to go when you are."

"I'll ask Sara to come along too. That way, we'll look like a family of tourists."

"It will still be tough getting close to that fortress. They must have guards patrolling the perimeter."

"They will, but there are ways to get in close without being noticed. Still, we won't take that risk unless I decide we have to. For now, I only want to gather more info."

"How will we do that if we don't risk getting closer?"

"We'll figure it out once we get there. And Sara might come up with an idea or two."

"She was an FBI agent once, right?"

"Yeah, and a private detective. Now she's interested in becoming a bounty hunter."

"I wouldn't want her chasing me. I'll bet she's relentless."

"That she is. And she tracked me down more than once years ago."

"Sara went after you back when she was an FBI agent?"

"That's right."

Henry laughed. "Well, she certainly did catch you. If not, you wouldn't be married."

"She's got me right where I want me," Cody said.

6
KIRK HYENA

KIRK HYENA HAD BEEN COLLECTING STAMPS SINCE HE WAS THREE. It had been a hobby of his father, his real father, and he'd continued it after being adopted.

As a boy he'd learned much about the world through the various stamps of other countries. Postage stamps were colorful, often portrayed scenes from a nation's history, and interesting facts about other cultures came to light while enjoying the hobby.

His adoptive father, Tristan Nilsson, also became interested in the hobby of philately, but only after he realized that the small pieces of paper could be used to launder illegal funds. Because of their diminutive size, rare stamps were handy to use in place of cash, which could be bulky in large sums.

Although Kirk had been preparing to kill the man someday and take over control of the country, he accelerated his plans to gain possession of a rare stamp. Nilsson had been using stamps for years to launder funds and Kirk hadn't been interested in any of them because he already owned them, or they were too common to appeal to him.

Then, remarkably, Nilsson gained possession of a stamp

known as the Inverted Jenny, a 24 cent United States postage stamp that was over a hundred years old. The stamp had an image of the Curtiss JN-4 airplane in the center of its design. The plane had been printed upside-down.

It was a rare stamp that Kirk had only seen photos of, and it was worth up to a million dollars or more, depending on what it would bring at an auction. Nilsson had plans to trade it for a shipment of heroin that he could cut and turn into two million.

Kirk couldn't allow that, and he'd ached to gain possession of the Inverted Jenny. He did just that after firing a bullet into the back of Tristan Nilsson's head.

He never liked the man and suspected he had something to do with his parents' fatal car accident. Kirk's birth father had been an accountant who'd worked for Nilsson at one time. Although he'd been very young, Kirk remembered a day when official-looking men in suits visited their house. He couldn't be sure, but he believed that his father had been pressured into helping authorities trap Nilsson or wear a wire.

Nilsson must have become aware of his father's true intentions and had the man killed, along with Kirk's mother. Kirk had no illusions about why Nilsson had adopted him and his brother, Niko, instead of letting them be sent off to an orphanage. No, that idea must have come from Nilsson's wife, Hannah.

Hannah Nilsson was incapable of having children. Kirk assumed that had been a mercy granted to the world by nature to keep the woman from breeding. Kirk had never understood why Nilsson had married Hannah. She had been a miserable bitch for whom nothing was ever good enough.

Although she lived amidst luxury in a land where many went to bed hungry, she always wanted more. One of her desires had been to be a mother, and so Kirk and his brother were given to her. When she wasn't ignoring them, she harangued them about everything they did. Her criticisms were always accompanied by the words, "If you were a real child of mine, you wouldn't be so stupid and worthless." The verbal abuse was often supplemented with a beating administered with the aid of a belt.

Kirk had given Niko the pleasure of killing her while he watched. Niko did so by beating her to death with a whip and echoing her words back at her.

"Who's stupid and worthless now? Hmm, bitch?"

As for the young twins, their deaths were a matter of necessity. They weren't just any orphans; they had been fathered by Tristan Nilsson with one of his lovers. When Kirk had stumbled upon that secret, he knew the children would have to die. The boy was Nilsson's pride and joy and would have been named as his heir eventually. Kirk couldn't have that, nor could he allow the boy to live and seek vengeance someday. The same was true of the girl.

They died in their sleep from the poison Kirk had slipped into the chocolate pudding they loved to eat. Apparently, one of the maids had been fond of the pudding, for she had been found dead the next day in her bed. Kirk thought it a fitting death for a food thief.

All went well after taking control of the country, but then foreign interests slipped in agitators, and they went to work on inciting the people.

Kirk faulted himself for not becoming aware of the problem sooner, but he'd been busy setting up relationships in South America and Europe that would have expanded their drug business. By the time he realized something was wrong, the rebels had infiltrated the staff of his home, which was a modern palace. An attempt was made on his life by a guard. Had it not been for his brother's quick reflexes, Kirk would have been shot to death while eating dinner.

As the traitorous guard drew his weapon and took aim, Niko had grabbed up a carving knife and flung it at the man. The blade embedded itself in the guard's chest and caused pain, but it didn't incapacitate him. He was about to shoot Niko when a second guard killed the man with a shot to the head. Their rescuer then yelled for Kirk and Niko to follow him to their living quarters. That guard, a man named Aroke, killed two more rebel guards and was wounded himself. Aroke was a native of the country and was the son of a man who had been Tristan Nilsson's personal bodyguard.

Aroke was Kirk's age and the three boys had grown up inside the palace together. Aroke stood six feet tall, had dusky skin, and large brown eyes that missed nothing. He'd always looked up to Kirk and the two were friends.

Months later, when they were forced to flee the country, Kirk took Aroke along with them. Other than his brother, Aroke was the only one Kirk trusted.

~

KIRK WAS IN HIS LIVING QUARTERS INSIDE THE ESTATE THAT doubled as a fortress. He was using a set of tongs to handle a new stamp he had recently acquired. It brought him joy to study the intricate artwork on the stamp.

When he heard a beep, he looked up at a set of monitors. The center one displayed a view of the corridor outside. Walking along the carpeted floor was Aroke. Kirk pressed a button that would release the lock on the door before Aroke needed to ring the bell for entry.

Aroke entered and took a seat across from Kirk. He was wearing a suit although he oversaw the guards. Kirk had told him that his days of being a uniformed guard ended when he'd saved his and his brother's lives.

Kirk asked a question as he was placing the stamp inside a glassine strip that would protect it. "What's on your mind, Aroke?"

"One of our people back home reported a rumor. A foreign government will be giving arms to the rebels."

"We expected that. Do they know which government it is?"

"No. But if I had to guess, I'd say it was the United States, or maybe the Chinese. Another rumor says that there will be an attempt on your life, and your brother's life soon."

Kirk nodded. "That's to be expected too. It's why I've locked myself up in here and sent Niko to that crypt in the desert. I'm confident that no assassin can get to either of us, and certainly not both of us."

"I am too, but it pays to be careful. Maybe you two should end any contact with the outside world."

"What contact? Oh, you mean the whores. I could do that for a month or two, but you might as well ask Niko to cut off one of his arms. If I stopped sending him women, he would do something foolish like leave the shelter and head into the city. If he didn't keep himself amused with his online gaming, he might have done that already."

"About the women, I've been told that he asks for the same one every time."

Kirk had been gazing down at a page of his stamp album. He looked up with a puzzled expression showing.

"The same girl? Has she been here?"

"No. I get your women from a different source. The ones Niko get are from a part of the city that's closer to his location. He was asking for a different girl every few days but then he began meeting with the same one. Her name is Delilah. I was told she has light skin, is very beautiful, and is only nineteen."

Kirk leaned back in his seat. "She must be fantastic in bed; I can't believe that Niko would fall in love with a whore."

"Do you want me to do something about it?"

"Like what?"

"I could tell her pimp to keep her away from Niko."

"No. If you did that, he might leave the shelter and go looking for her. Do nothing for now and let my brother have his fun. No matter how good this girl is in bed, Niko will tire of her soon."

"I guess you're right."

"What about that other habit of his?"

"He's still doing it."

Kirk shook his head. "I thought he was smarter than that."

"He's intelligent, but he's also impulsive."

"I need to make him see how dangerous his behavior is."

"I can help with that."

"Do so. Maybe he'll learn a lesson. Is there anything else I should know about?"

"There's a holiday coming up here soon. It's called Our Lady of Guadalupe Day. The men are going to want to go into town to celebrate. It will be better to let them have the time off in shifts than to deny them."

"Isn't that a religious holiday?"

"Yes. It has something to do with the Virgin Mary."

Kirk laughed. "These murderous cartel thugs are religious?"

"Some are. But I think they're more interested in enjoying the feasting that will be going on. It will also give them a break from their duties."

"That means we'll have less men here than usual during that time. If I was an assassin, that might be when I would attack."

"I know. But I'll only let half of the men go into town at any one time, that way, we'll still have about two dozen guards here."

Kirk looked thoughtful for a moment as he tapped his fingers on the desk. "I've got a better idea. Tell the men they can all have two days in the city. That way, they can let off some steam, get drunk, and still have time to recover."

Aroke looked stunned by the suggestion. "You want to leave yourself defenseless?"

"Of course not. But I won't be here. During that time, I'll visit my brother in his underground hideout. I miss him, and maybe I'll get a look at this hooker of his."

"I'll go with you when you travel, but I'll assign a man to check on the estate once a day. Before you return, we should also have it swept for listening devices or bombs."

"Good idea, but they'd have to be a magician to get over the wall," Kirk said, as he reached for a satellite phone that was on the desk. "I'll call Niko and let him know he'll be having company soon."

7

NIKO HYENA

NIKO HYENA PLACED HIS SATELLITE PHONE ON THE NIGHTSTAND next to his bed after speaking to his brother.

A naked young woman emerged from the connected bathroom at his left and grinned at him. Her name was Delilah. She had luminous brown eyes, flawless skin, generous curves, and dark curly hair cascaded down her back. She spoke to Niko in English, a language they both understood. Delilah had learned the language as a child from one of her mother's boyfriends. He had been an American who had lived with them for years before returning to the United States.

"Was that your brother?"

"Yeah. Kirk will be coming here soon."

Delilah crawled into bed beside Niko. She was not working but was seeing him on her own time. That had been Niko's idea, and Delilah had agreed.

Delilah ran a hand over Niko's muscular chest. "Is your brother like you?"

Niko smiled. "Not really. I'm the brawn and he's the brains. We make a great team. I'll be glad to see him again. This is the first time we've been separated since we were children."

"I have a little brother, but I also had two sisters. They were both killed three years ago when some narcos were shooting at each other. I almost died too. One of the bullets passed through my hair. It was so close to my skull that it hurt me, even though it never touched me."

"It was the kinetic force of the round."

"What?"

"When the bullet passed through your hair it compressed the air around it. You must have felt the force of the compressed air being slammed against your head."

Delilah smiled at Niko. "You're smart."

"Not really."

Delilah touched the thick bracelet Niko wore. "What is this?"

The bracelet was black and displayed a green light that was diamond shaped. It was the device that monitored his brother's pulse through a satellite link. Kirk wore a similar bracelet that kept track of Niko's pulse. If the light on Niko's bracelet turned red and began beeping, it would signify that Kirk was dead and that Niko should flee the bunker. Likewise, if the light on Kirk's bracelet turned red, it would mean that Niko had died.

"This bracelet contains a link that helps me know my brother is safe."

"Is he inside another bunker somewhere?"

"No, but he is being guarded."

"Why does someone want to hurt you two?"

Niko decided to change the subject. "How old were your sisters?"

"One was eighteen and the other was eleven. I still miss them."

Niko ran a hand over Delilah's naked hip. "I bet they were beautiful if they were related to you."

"They were. And my older sister was gorgeous. She looked like me, but her father was an American, and she had gotten his blue eyes. I wish I had those eyes."

Niko leaned over and kissed Delilah. "I wouldn't change a thing about you."

~

Hours later, it was time for Delilah to leave. For that to happen, Niko had to first deactivate certain security measures, such as the land mines that were near the shelter's entrance. Those mines were set to go off if more than sixty pounds of pressure were detected. They could also be activated by remote control. If the mines failed, there were machine guns nearby that would activate.

The entrance was built into solid rock. It was camouflaged by fake stone that covered steel doors that could be slid aside. To reach the inner chamber of the shelter, one had to pass through three separate sets of two-inch thick steel doors.

If someone breached the first door, they would be gassed and rendered unconscious. If they survived that, perhaps with the aid of a gas mask and oxygen, they would be targeted by four hidden rifles that were controlled by a computer within the next chamber. They would be shot with more than a hundred rounds before they could hope to breach the third door. If by some miracle they managed to survive and do that, they would enter the inner chamber only to have the floor give way beneath them and would fall fifteen feet onto sharp metal spikes.

Once Niko was certain there was no one near the entrance, he escorted Delilah to the outer doors and kissed her goodbye. He had put on sneakers and running shorts but wore no shirt.

Niko opened the first of the three doors and Delilah entered the small chamber. The door slid close behind her three seconds before the next one slid open. That process repeated with the final door and Delilah stepped outside.

She had a red motor scooter parked within the shade of a small hill. As she rode away while waving goodbye at the hidden cameras she knew were there, Niko waved back at her and felt a tug at his heart.

He kept telling himself he wasn't falling in love with Delilah, but it hurt him more each time they separated. The fact that she would be with other men upset him, but he refused to admit it. If he acknowledged his jealousy, he would then have to recognize the love that spawned it.

He opened the first door again when he could no longer see her on the cameras. A minute later, Niko was standing at the exit and looking out at the barren landscape. He remained in full view outside the bunker's entrance for several minutes despite the risk. He enjoyed breathing in the fresh air and was in no hurry to reenter the bunker. And even though it was hot and humid outside, the breeze revitalized him. If not for Delilah and his video games, he would have gone crazy over the last few weeks.

And thank God there was a gym down in the bunker. Although, Niko disliked running on a treadmill. To avoid it and still get in his cardio, he began taking chances with his life by running in the desert. He knew if his brother found out about it that he would think he was insane.

After walking beyond the entrance until he spotted a mark indicating he was at a safe distance, Niko withdrew a remote control from his pocket and pressed a button. Slabs of fake stone slid back into place to conceal the bunker's entrance as the locks reactivated with a clicking sound. The land mines had also been activated.

Confident that no one could enter the bunker during his absence, Niko began running in the opposite direction that Delilah had taken. The area had hills and sand dunes that presented a challenge and got his heart racing. When he reached a far set of hills that bordered a small valley with a flat plain, he would turn around and head back. After the first mile he was sweating and smiling as he felt the sun on his back.

He was aware that people wanted him dead, but he also doubted they knew where he was. Besides, he didn't like living in a hole in the ground. Going for a run four or five times a week wasn't a risk since there was rarely anyone around other than the occasional hiker. Or so Niko thought.

As he topped a hill while breathing with his mouth open, he found a man waiting for him. The man wore a mask and was holding a gun. Niko skidded to a halt, held up a hand, and made a strangled cry as the man raised the weapon and took aim at his head.

"Bang!" the man said. "You're dead."

Niko gawked at him, then realized that he recognized his voice. "Aroke?"

Aroke removed his mask and held out his other hand. There was a satellite phone in it. "Your brother would like to speak with you."

Niko grunted in anger and snatched the phone from Aroke's hand. "Kirk? What the hell, man? Aroke almost gave me a heart attack."

"And you would no longer have a heartbeat if he had been a real assassin. Niko, what are you thinking by running outside? Do you want to get killed?"

"I hate running on a treadmill, you know that. And I need some fresh air once in a while."

"Niko, I know being in the bunker isn't fun, but we have to be careful or we'll both be killed. I spend most of my time in one room these days. But if we're cautious and stay patient, we'll be back home and running things again. Use the treadmill, jump rope, run in place, or just sit still, but you can't risk yourself by leaving the bunker. It's dangerous enough that you have whores visiting you there."

"How is that a risk?"

"It's a risk every time you open the door for someone. Their comings and goings also leave behind tracks in the sand; tracks that lead right to you."

"So what? That's why there are the land mines and the other defenses."

"I know. But there are men out there who might find a way around such things. Remember Maurice Scallato? If he'd been hired to kill you, he could have done it. And that other assassin, Tanner, he could probably do it."

"Bullshit! Tanner is just lucky. I hope he is hired to kill me. I would love to avenge Maurice by killing him."

"Really?"

"Yes."

"Then why are you making it so easy for him to kill you by running around the desert unarmed?"

Niko sighed. "I hear you, Kirk, and I'll stop running, but no way am I giving up Delilah, um, I mean, the whores. I'd go nuts if I didn't have a woman for weeks."

"I won't ask you to give that up. And who is this Delilah, one of the prostitutes?"

"Yes. She's my favorite."

"Enjoy her, and the other women too. And stay patient, brother. We'll be in control again soon and then these long days will be a bad memory."

Niko smiled into the phone. "I'm looking forward to seeing you, and bring me something when you come to visit."

"What would you like?"

"Some real chow would be nice; I could use a break from the freeze-dried food and frozen dinners. And bring me something sweet. Remember that chocolate cake Mrs. Crowley used to make for us. Damn, I miss that cake. I can't believe Mrs. Crowley ran out on us."

"I'll bring you food and I'll bring you a chocolate cake. It won't be as good as Mrs. Crowley's, but it will be close. Be smart and stay inside the bunker, okay?"

"I will."

"Good. Now, let me talk to Aroke."

Niko handed Aroke back his phone. Aroke listened, said, "Okay," then listened again before saying goodbye and ending the call.

"Kirk wants me to stay with you until you're back inside the bunker."

Niko punched Aroke on the shoulder. "You scared the shit out of me, asshole."

Aroke smiled. "Then my plan worked."

They walked back to the entrance of the bunker with Niko asking questions.

"How did you get here? I never saw a vehicle."

"I parked a pickup truck three miles away and walked in."

"And how did you know where I would be?"

"It was easy. I followed the tracks you made on your last run and found a good spot to wait for you."

"Okay, but what if I hadn't gone for a run today?"

"I would have kept returning until I came across you."

"What? And just stood out here waiting?"

"Yes."

Niko laughed. "And I thought my days were boring."

Once they'd reached the bunker, Aroke stayed back beyond the field of land mines. Niko called to him from the open doorway. "Tell my brother I'll be a good boy from now on and stay inside."

"Running on a treadmill can give you just as good a workout as running outside."

Niko gave Aroke the finger then hit a button on a wall that would close the outer doors and seal him inside the bunker. As he walked deeper into the chamber, Niko realized he missed Delilah.

8

FUN ACROSS THE BORDER

Cody had been considering which Hyena brother to take a contract on when he remembered that Spenser had recently mentioned something to him concerning rare stamps.

When he contacted his mentor to ask him about it, Spenser told him about one of his former clients. Spenser was no longer an assassin. Instead, he made a living by helping people who were being threatened. His sort of assistance was required when the police weren't enough. Unlike the cops, Spenser wasn't constrained by a set of laws or rules. He would kill to protect a client and did so quite often. His compensation didn't come from his clients but from their victimizers. Once they were dead, Spenser would gain possession of their money and other assets, if they had any. Sometimes there was nothing to be had. In such instances, he still never charged the client.

One of his clients was a collector of rare stamps and had been threatened by a man who blamed him for the death of his daughter. The man had been in prison for bank robbery when his daughter had been struck and killed by the vehicle Spenser's client had been driving.

The client had been found innocent of wrongdoing because the young woman he'd struck had run out into the road while out of her mind on drugs. That had been nine years earlier, and the client had put the horrible incident behind him.

The father of the dead woman had not. When he was released from prison, he began a campaign of terror against Spenser's client. Because he always wore a mask and had friends who would offer an alibi for his whereabouts, there was nothing the police could do.

The same was not true for Spenser. Spenser caught the ex-con in the act as he was attempting to set fire to his client's vacation cabin. He saved the man's life and that of the man's own daughter, and his wife. As was true of most of Spenser's grateful clients, the man told Spenser he owed him a favor.

"I may need you to cash-in on that favor for me, Spenser."

"What's up?"

While sitting at the desk in his office, Cody went on to tell Spenser about the two contracts, along with the detail that Kirk Hyena was a collector of rare stamps. Spenser gave him information about the stamp his client possessed.

"His most valuable stamp is something called a 2-cent Hawaiian Missionary. I've seen it. It was blue, and it had some sort of curlicue artwork around the border and the number two in its center. I think it's worth close to a million and there are only about a dozen of them in the world."

"That would be a tempting bit of bait for a man like Kirk Hyena. Still, I'm not sure it's enough to make him come out of hiding to risk his life."

"It sounds like you've decided on which brother to go after."

"I haven't yet, no, but if I'm going to hand one of these contracts off to someone, I'll also want to offer them as much information as I can gather, along with a suggestion on how to kill them."

"About the stamp, my client might not be willing to take a chance of losing it. He owes me, but that would be asking a lot of him."

"He wouldn't have to risk it. With the plan I have in mind, the stamp would never leave his possession."

"Ah, you only need Kirk Hyena to think you have it."

"Yeah, and maybe he'd be willing to leave that fortress to get his hands on it. If so, he couldn't show up to make the deal with an army of cartel thugs around him, not if he wanted to portray himself as a solid citizen worthy of selling the stamp to."

"It sounds like something that might work. But what about the other brother?"

"That one will be tougher. I'll know more by the time I return from Mexico. I also have a hacker looking into ways to override that bunker's security system."

"Damn, Cody. You're making me wish I was still an assassin; they're both interesting and challenging targets."

"One of them is yours if you want it, Spenser."

"Thanks, but I'll have to pass. I never know when a former client will recommend me to one of their friends who are in trouble. When that happens, I need to be ready to react. I will be there for you if you need me, you know that, boy."

"I do, and the same goes for me."

"Let me know if you'll need me to talk to my client who has the rare stamp."

"I will, and thanks, Spenser."

"You're welcome, and give my love to Sara and the children."

"Will do."

After getting off the phone, Cody went upstairs to pack for his trip to Mexico, since they were flying out in the morning. Sara was coming along, and Franny would be looking after the children for a few days. Lucas and Marian hadn't been happy about being left behind, but they cheered up when Cody told them they would be going to New York City soon.

"How soon?" Lucas had asked.

"After the holidays are over."

"You mean next year?"

"Yeah."

"Daddy, that's a long way off."

Cody had smiled at him and remembered when as a child he too thought that an event a few weeks out was a long way off.

"It will get here sooner than you think, and if it snows, we'll go sledding in Central Park like we did last year."

That promise made Lucas smile. He had loved sledding down hills the winter before.

Marian had sat on her father's lap and asked him to bring her something back from Mexico.

"Like what?"

"One of those big hats... an umbrello."

"I think you mean sombrero."

Marian nodded, making her golden hair shimmer. "Yeah, Daddy. I want a red one."

"I'll see what I can do."

Marian kissed him. "That means I'll get one."

~

CODY WAS DOWN IN THE GYM WORKING OUT WITH WEIGHTS WHEN he received a call from Tim Jackson. He lowered the barbell he'd been curling, sat on the edge of a weight bench, and took the call.

Tim reported that he'd had no luck finding a way into the security system inside the underground bunker.

"I'm guessing it's an isolated system, so no joy there, but I was able to get close to your target."

"What? How?"

"He's a serious gamer and so am I. Niko Hyena uses the name Cutthroat when he plays online. And man is he ever good."

"When you play, are you all onscreen?"

"At times, but Niko uses an avatar and so do I."

"Good. That means he won't know what you look like. The risk would be low to you if he did, but any risk would be too much."

"There's something else."

"Yeah?"

"I couldn't get into his security system, but I think I might be able to hack the satellite phone he uses. If I can, I'll start sending you recordings of his conversations."

"That would be great, Tim. As usual, you're doing fantastic work. I'll be in Mexico for a few days, hold on and I'll give you the number you can reach me at. I'll be using the name Thomas Myers."

"Gotcha. And have a good trip."

"I plan to," Cody said.

∼

THE NEXT DAY, CODY WAS IN CIUDAD JUÁREZ, MEXICO, WITH Sara and Henry. Sara's passport had her last name listed as Myers, and so did Henry's. The passports were real. That was one of the perks of working with Thomas Lawson.

Cody was wearing the special glasses that had been designed to counteract facial recognition software by changing the contours of a face. The lenses had the added advantage of taming his intense eyes.

He didn't want to run the risk of being recognized and would act like he was a tourist on vacation. And they were on vacation to some degree. Although he and Henry would be spending time doing surveillance on the two sites where the Hyena brothers were, that wouldn't take all their time. The truth was that Cody had low expectations on learning anything vital. However, the chance did exist, and he would be foolish to not make the effort.

Spenser once told him something during his training that his grandfather had already drummed into him when he was a boy growing up on the ranch.

Walter Parker, Cody's grandfather, had been a wise man, and he had learned well from most of the mistakes he'd made during his life, along with the mistakes made by others.

After Cody had come in third during a shooting competition when he was ten years old, he was sad, because he'd thought he should have done better.

"You're right," Walter told him, as he drove Cody home in his pickup truck. "And you would have done better if you had practiced more."

"I didn't think I needed to."

"You're a hell of a good shot, Cody, and it comes natural to you. But that don't mean you can sit on your butt and not give it your all. If you had practiced more, I bet you would have won that competition."

"I'll win the next one."

"Why will it be any different next time?"

"Because I'm going to practice more, and I'm going to start as soon as we get back home to the ranch."

His grandfather had smiled at him. "That's what I want to hear. And now you listen, boy. You give it everything you've got. That way, if you lose, you know that you did your best. And I'll tell you a secret too."

"What secret?"

"If you really do your best, no one is likely to beat you at anything. Most people go through life at half speed, but you're a Parker, Cody, and that means you're a winner."

Cody held up the small third place trophy he'd been given. "I wasn't a winner today."

"The hell you aren't. You're my grandson and I love you. You'll always be a winner in my eyes, boy, even if you couldn't hit the side of a barn."

Cody had told his grandfather that he loved him too, and he never again did anything he deemed important without giving it his all.

If he learned nothing on his trip to Mexico, he would at least know that he had made the attempt to gain intelligence before committing to a target.

Cody, Sara, and Henry checked into a 4-star hotel that had spacious suites and an indoor swimming pool. There was no language barrier since all three of them could speak and read Spanish, also, most of the staff of the hotel spoke English, and they were professional and courteous.

They had arrived at the hotel in a pair of black Jeeps that Cody had arranged to have the use of through Lawson. They weren't rentals and they couldn't be traced back to them. The keys to the Jeeps had been given to Cody by a white man wearing a green suit with a yellow tie. The man also handed him a package that contained three guns and a box of ammunition. The acquiring of weapons had likewise been arranged by Thomas Lawson. Cody would dispose of the weapons before flying home if he had to use them. He didn't think he would need them since he wasn't planning to make a run at either target, but it paid to be careful and ready to respond to violence.

It was evening by the time they were settled in the hotel, and Cody made the decision to wait until morning to start surveillance on the fortress. In the meantime, they could explore the city and have dinner.

Juarez had experienced much violence in the recent past as two rival cartels vied for control of the drug business in the area. Currently, Juarez was safer. In fact, there was less violence taking place than in many U.S. cities. That's quite a change considering the city had once averaged about six murders a day for years.

After eating dinner with them, Henry went off on his own to explore the nightlife. Sara watched him walk away with a worried expression.

"Maybe he shouldn't be alone."

Cody smiled. "Henry will be fine. He hasn't finished his training yet, but he's deadlier with his hands than any three men he's ever likely to meet, and he's also armed."

"He's still only nineteen."

"Yeah, but he's always been smarter than average and mature for his age. He won't get into trouble by doing anything stupid."

"I know you're right. It just felt odd watching him walk off like that."

"Think how you'll feel when Lucas goes off on his own someday."

Sara moaned. "I don't want to think about that."

Cody took her by the hand while flagging down a taxi in front of the restaurant. "C'mon, let's go have some fun of our own."

"What do you have in mind?"

Cody smiled at her. "I want to dance with my wife."

~

Before heading to Juarez, Cody had explored the city online. Sara had been a fan of heavy metal music when she was a teen growing up in Connecticut. Cody had come across a nightclub that had a band that performed the heavy metal music from that time and wanted to surprise his wife by going there.

The bar was crowded and at least half of the people on the dance floor were Americans from across the Rio Grande in El Paso.

Cody thought he might be the oldest one there, but he spied a few men and women who were older than he was. Not that he felt old being in his early forties, but he knew that most dance clubs catered to a younger crowd.

Despite his age, he was as fit as anyone else, and dancing was a good exercise. Sara was excited to be at the club and was thrilled to be hearing the music she loved when she was a teen. The band was great, and the singers did an excellent job of mimicking the original vocalists of the songs.

Cody wasn't a fan of heavy metal music but did enjoy some of it, and he was familiar with the tunes because Romeo had often played the music during the road trips they had taken together as young assassins. The music was secondary. His pleasure came from watching his wife have a good time. They danced off and on for hours before returning to their hotel, where they made love in the suite's large shower.

After getting only three hours of sleep, Cody rose from bed and slipped out of their suite. Playtime was over, and it was time to go to work.

9

GATHERING INTEL

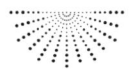

Cody had made plans to meet Henry in the hotel's coffee shop at five a.m. He was headed there at 4:53 when he saw Henry enter the hotel. Henry spotted him as well and walked over to him.

"Since you're wearing the same clothes you had on last night, I'll assume you've made a friend and had a good time."

Henry grinned. "Her name is Bianca. I'll be having dinner with her later."

"Do you want to take time to shower and change clothes? I can order our food to go and meet you in the parking garage."

"That would be great," Henry said. "But I don't want to hold you up."

"We've got time. We'll also be stopping for gas and supplies on the way. We may be out in the desert for most of the day and we'll need water."

"Okay. Cool. I'll meet you down in the garage in fifteen minutes."

Henry rushed toward the elevators and Cody went inside the coffee shop to order breakfast sandwiches. He was pleased to see they had thermoses for sale but decided not to buy them because they had the hotel's name on them. If he or Henry had to leave one behind for some reason, the thermos would lead anyone hoping to find them right to their door.

Cody arrived at the Jeeps with the sandwiches and two cups of coffee to find that Henry had been true to his word. He expected nothing less from a future Tanner. He was also pleased to see that Henry was dressed as he was, in khaki pants and an earth tone shirt that was a shade of beige. The muted colors would help them to blend in with the desert landscape.

Cody handed Henry his sandwich and drink. Henry walked over to the passenger door, but then Cody pointed at the vehicle Henry was using. "I think we'll take both Jeeps."

"Why?"

"Two reasons: First, we'll be going out to an area where the conditions are harsh, if one Jeep breaks down, we'll still have the other. And the second reason is because we might need to separate at some point."

"That makes sense, and no matter what, it gives us options we wouldn't have with only one vehicle."

"Exactly."

~

CODY LED THE WAY AND DROVE WHILE TAKING BITES FROM HIS sandwich. When they stopped for gas at a station that had a convenience store, he bought two cases of bottled water, two foam coolers, ice, and cold sandwiches. On a whim, he threw in two packs of cupcakes for a treat. Some of the water would go to waste because it would be dropped off along the route they used to walk closer to the estate. If for whatever reason they were left stranded in the desert, they would have a few bottles of water each to sustain themselves.

Cody took such precautions whenever he entered a desert environment. Doing so had been a part of his training, and now it was Henry's turn to acquire the habit. Such practices could someday mean the difference between life and death, or success and failure. A Tanner couldn't afford to fail nor had one ever done so.

Cody was heading to the counter to pay for everything when he spotted a red sombrero. The hat was perfect for Marian and was kid-size. Not wanting to overlook Lucas, he grabbed a small, colorful poncho from a rack. Before leaving Mexico, he would also buy a gift for Franny, along with something for the dog, Lucky. The hound seemed to mope if gifts were given out and he wasn't included.

∼

THEY REACHED THE AREA NEAR THE ESTATE CODY THOUGHT OF AS the fortress. They were miles away from it but could make out details thanks to the zoom capabilities of their digital cameras.

Cody had found a spot on a hill that allowed a good vantage point for viewing the gate built into the wall surrounding the property. Along with the gate there was a guard shack.

Several guards were on patrol outside the wall. The camera zoomed in so close to them that Cody could almost make out their features.

"This camera is incredible," Henry said.

"I'm glad you like it. Consider it an early Christmas present."

"Thanks. And for your present, I'd like to find a way to get to one of these targets."

"I would like that gift, but for now, I'm just gathering intelligence for when we return to make the hit."

"Hey, look over to the right. There's a vehicle coming down the road that leads to the estate. It looks like a minivan."

Cody zoomed in on the van but was unable to make out the writing that was on the side of it. He needed to get a new angle on it.

"Stay here. I'm going to move in closer and see if I can get a better shot of that van. It looks like there's some sort of sign on its side."

"I'll keep watching the guards. If it looks like they've spotted you while you change position, I'll let you know."

Cody moved in a low crouch. He wore a beige cap on his head so his dark hair wouldn't stand out against the desert's landscape.

After covering over a quarter of a mile, Cody laid flat and used the camera again. The vehicle had reached the gate by then and four guards with rifles were there to meet it. The camera revealed that six women and a man were getting out of the van. Four of the women were thick-set, and the man had white hair. Cody concluded that they were there to work. The van had a name written on it, but the lettering was still too small to make out. Cody considered moving closer, then nixed that idea because he didn't want to press his luck.

The women and the old man were escorted through a steel door that was next to a guard shack. From where he was before, Cody had been unable to make out the door. Getting through a door would be easier than scaling a wall. There was also no way to know what lay beyond that door. No alarms sounded as the van approached the estate; that meant the sensors in the walls had been disabled from within. If Cody decided to go over the wall to get to Kirk Hyena, doing so while the van approached would be a good time to make such a move.

Cody took out his phone to send off a text to Henry. He wanted to ask him to move closer to the road at a spot that was farther away from the fortress. That way, he might be able to get near enough to read the sign on the side of the van. Unfortunately, there was no cell service where he was, and the text failed to go through.

The van drove back along the road after dropping off its passengers and moved away from the estate at a good speed. Cody paused to try once again to read the sign on its side, but it was no use.

Concern for Henry drove the van from his mind when he returned to the hill to find that Henry was gone. His apprehension vanished when he saw that his apprentice had left him a note written in the sand.

I'm moving closer to get a better look at that van.

Cody smiled. Henry hadn't needed to be told what to do; he had figured it out for himself. That was a good sign. In the years ahead, when he was acting on his own, there would be no one there to do his thinking for him. If he was going to be a Tanner, he'd have to be a self-starter and able to think on his feet.

Cody met the teen as he was coming back. Henry didn't see him at first because he had his camera zoomed in on the guards who were visible. When Henry noticed him, Cody could tell by the smile on his face that he'd been successful.

"You got close enough to make out the sign?"

"I did. It had the words, Lopez Transport: We Move People and Things, written on it in Spanish, and I even got the license plate and a fuzzy photo of the driver's face."

"Good work."

Henry's grin grew wider at the praise, then he pointed toward the area where they'd left the Jeeps. "I'm thirsty. I'll hike to my Jeep and bring back some water."

"We'll both go, and we'll leave here. I want to get a look at the terrain where that bunker is located."

"Yeah, me too. I know the estate is an interesting challenge because it's guarded by dozens of men and has that wall around it, but if I had to choose a target, I'd go after that bunker."

"Why?"

"Because it's a mystery. I love solving mysteries."

"You might get the chance to help me solve it, but before I decide which contract to take, I need more info."

They were back at their vehicles and downing bottles of water when Henry stopped drinking and sent Cody a worried look.

"What's wrong?"

"That message I left you in the sand. I forgot to erase it

before we left. If one of the guards came across it, they would know we were there."

"We're good; I erased it after reading it."

"Oh, I should have known you would."

"No. It's good that you didn't assume it. In this line of work, you may only get to make a mistake once."

"We still left tracks behind."

"Yeah, but that can't be helped, and it's unlikely that any guard will travel that far from the estate. It's why I brought the cameras. That zoom feature allows us to watch them without risking ourselves unnecessarily."

"If you do decide to go after Kirk Hyena, how will you do it?"

"If he's my target, I don't plan to go after him inside that estate. If possible, I'll make him come to me."

Henry nodded in understanding. "You're talking about that stamp you told me about."

"That's right. If he's as big a fanatic about stamps as I think he is, a chance to get his hands on that rare stamp might be enough to make him risk himself by leaving the estate."

"Are you counting on that?"

"No. But I'd like to avoid going inside that fortress if I can. It would be much better to tempt Kirk Hyena to leave it."

"And what about Niko Hyena? Is there a way to get him to leave that bunker?"

"That's a good question. Let's go have a look at Niko's hole in the ground."

∼

THEY USED THE CAMERAS AGAIN AT NIKO'S UNDERGROUND hideaway, but since there were no patrolling guards, Cody decided to move in closer. When they did, they spotted the tracks left behind in the sand by the scooter Delilah rode. They had seen tracks from other vehicles scattered about the area but none of the others were as close to the bunker.

Cody studied Delilah's tracks. "Some of these look recent. I think Niko might have a regular visitor who rides a motorcycle."

Henry laughed. "Maybe he orders pizza."

They followed the tracks as they grew closer to where they thought the entrance to the bunker might be located, then they used the cameras again. The tracks ended near the base of a rocky hill.

"That must be the entrance, and it looks like the area shown in the photos Lawson gave me."

"What now?" Henry asked.

"We wait and watch," Cody said as he pointed to the bottom of the hill. To his eye, it looked as if changes had been made to the natural landscape in that area. "Lawson's people assumed that there are numerous cameras, sensor plates, land mines, and possibly automated machine gun nests protecting the bunker's entrance. I think they were right. Some of those protrusions near the base of that hill don't look natural to me because they're spaced evenly apart. They're probably concealed cameras and guns."

"I guess we'd better not get any closer, huh?"

"I wouldn't risk it. Let's settle in and wait to see if anything happens."

∼

ONE HOUR AND FORTY-EIGHT MINUTES LATER, IT WAS HENRY WHO heard the motor of Delilah's scooter first. This time, they were already close enough to take a photo of the license plate, thanks to the zoom lens.

Delilah halted her scooter along the base of a hill, got off it, and waved toward a rock wall that was forty yards away.

When Cody saw Henry cock his head, he knew the boy had heard something. Henry had exceptional hearing and often detected sounds he couldn't.

"What is it? Did you hear something?"

"Yeah, a clicking noise."

Seconds later, they watched through the cameras as the fake walls of stone slid aside. Delilah removed her helmet and her long hair spilled across her shoulders and down her back.

"She's hot," Henry whispered.

"That she is. Do you see Niko?"

"No, but it looks like she's talking to someone, but I can't make out her words, or his. And the guy's voice sounds like it's coming from an intercom."

"I can't hear them at all; you've got some ears on you."

"Grandma used to say I could hear a flea fart from a mile away."

Cody was keeping an eye on the entrance to the bunker while wishing he had a scoped rifle instead of a zoom camera. It was possible that Niko might be foolish enough to expose himself.

That didn't happen, and a moment later Delilah walked into the entrance and disappeared. Then, the fake walls of stone slid into place, sealing the entrance.

"I heard that click sound again," Henry said. "Maybe it's the locks engaging and disengaging."

"It could be."

"That girl might be the key to killing Niko. He has to open up the bunker to let her in and out."

"Yeah, but if we'd been much closer, I'm betting his security system would have detected us. Still, it is a weakness, and any weakness in a defense can be exploited."

"What's next? Do we stay here, or should we go back to check out the fortress again?"

"We'll stay here, but I want you to head back to your Jeep and be ready to follow that woman when she comes out. I want to know who she is, although I can guess."

"You think she's a hooker?"

"Yeah. Although it's possible Niko has a girlfriend no one

knew about. This is good, Henry. We have more info than we had this morning. Now, I need to think of a way to use it."

Henry went off at a jog to return to his vehicle to wait for Delilah.

Hours passed. They were hours wherein the temperature rose, and Cody found himself sweating. Finally, the stone walls separated, and Delilah emerged from the bunker. Before leaving, she sent a wave toward the hidden cameras, then rode off.

Cody watched for another half hour before hiking back to his Jeep. He had decided to drive back to the area where the estate was located. He wanted to see if the people who had been dropped off that morning were also picked up in the evening. If so, the transport van might be used to breach the fortress's defenses.

A text came in from Henry while Cody was on the highway. It stated that he had followed Delilah back to Juarez and that she lived in an apartment building that was about a twenty-minute drive away from their hotel.

Cody texted him back. He let Henry know he had done good work and that he could have the rest of the day off.

Once he was back at his spy post near the estate, Cody settled in and kept watch. At around six o'clock, the same van returned to pick up the household staff and ferry them back to the city. Cody left the area as well and headed to his hotel.

It had been a productive day and he now knew more about both targets. That knowledge hadn't helped him to decide which of the Hyena brothers to kill. He wanted them both, but since he couldn't be in two places at once, he'd have to make a choice eventually.

One thing was certain; whoever he chose, they would die. No other outcome was possible given that he was a Tanner.

10

IMPULSIVE

The apartment house Henry had followed Delilah to was where she lived with her mother and younger brother, Tomás.

The boy was nine and small for his age, but he was the best soccer player in his neighborhood. He'd been playing the game outside with friends when Delilah had come home. She'd become a prostitute out of desperation for money to keep herself and her brother from winding up on the streets. Before that, Delilah had been going to school to become a nurse while working part-time as a sales clerk.

Her mother was an alcoholic who drank every peso she got her hands on. By the time Delilah found out they were behind on the rent and in danger of being evicted, they were deep in a financial hole. She'd been selling herself for weeks when she'd met Niko Hyena. She had been as attracted to him as he was to her, and she had trouble getting Niko out of her mind.

Henry hadn't followed Delilah inside the building, but he had seen her give her little brother a kiss on the cheek before entering and overheard her asking about their mother. Tomás had replied that their mother was sleeping. Delilah knew that meant that their mother was drunk again.

After receiving Cody's reply, Henry had driven off. He was

looking forward to seeing Bianca again and the time for their date was approaching. Had he entered the building, Henry would have witnessed a scene of violence.

∼

Delilah had been about to climb the stairs up to her third-floor apartment when a hulking figure stepped out of the shadows and asked her where she'd been.

"Hernando? You scared me."

"I said, where have you been?"

"I was… visiting a friend."

Hernando smiled and revealed the two gold teeth he had. "Does this friend of yours live out in the desert? Because that's where you've been. And if you've been there, that means you owe me money."

"I'm not working today."

Hernando's slap was swift and knocked Delilah off her feet. As she laid on the dirty hallway floor feeling stunned, he leaned over and spoke in a cold and menacing tone.

"Your ass is mine. You belong to me, and whenever you fuck someone, I expect to get paid."

Delilah touched a corner of her mouth, and her fingers came away wet with blood. She was afraid of Hernando, but seeing the blood had angered her, as she felt she had done nothing to deserve a beating.

"I have never cheated you, Hernando. When Niko pays me, I give you the money… but I like him. I won't charge him every time I see him."

Hernando's nostrils flared as he gritted his teeth. His next blow wasn't a slap. It was a solid punch delivered to Delilah's left eye. More blows followed amid shouted curses. By the time Hernando ended his assault with a kick to her ribs, Delilah had already been rendered unconscious.

∾

THAT NIGHT, HERNANDO WAS AT HIS FAVORITE NIGHTCLUB AND having drinks with a woman who believed he was a sales manager. In a way he was, since he was a pimp. The woman was a lawyer who specialized in real estate contracts. She'd grown up in a well-to-do family in Mexico City. Despite his profession, Hernando had always been attracted to women with class.

The people near the entrance became quiet and then separated to let someone through. It was Delilah. Her bruised and battered face was puffy, and her left eye was swollen closed. She was not alone, and when she spotted Hernando with her one good eye, she pointed him out to her companion, a muscular white man.

Hernando was reaching for the knife he kept sheathed to his belt when the man grabbed him by his tie and lifted him off his stool as if he weighed no more than a child.

The tie was choking him, but it became a secondary concern to Hernando after the first punch landed. The blows had such force that Hernando had to struggle to stay conscious. His face was reddening, and he was gasping for air when his assailant released him, and he collapsed onto the nightclub's floor. Then the kicking began. Each kick broke a rib, a bone, or damaged a tooth. By the time the thrashing ended, Hernando was out cold and had a collapsed lung; two broken arms; missing teeth; and a dislocated jaw. Before leaving, his attacker made it a point to send a hard kick against Hernando's crotch. Several of the men watching moaned as they imagined what such an assault had done to Hernando's testicles.

As brutal as it was, the beating had been performed in seventeen seconds. Twenty seconds after that, the perpetrator was back inside his car with Delilah and headed away from the bar. The man's name was Niko Hyena.

∾

Cody had been having a late dinner with Sara at a restaurant inside the hotel when he received a call from Henry. He could tell by the noise in the background that Henry was someplace where a lot of people were present. He wondered if something was wrong when he heard the sound of a siren gaining in volume.

"Henry, are you all right?"

"I'm good, but I have a photo to send you. Call me back and tell me if it's who I think it is."

Cody waited for the photo to come through. When it did, he saw a side view of a man's face that was reddened with rage. The photo appeared to have been taken in a bar and the man was Niko Hyena.

Cody called Henry back. "You saw Niko?"

"Oh man, did I ever. I was walking along the street with my date when I spotted that girl we saw earlier at the bunker, only her face was a wreck, like someone beat her. Then I noticed she wasn't alone and that there was a man with her—Niko."

"Why does he look so angry in the photo? And is that a police car I hear in the background?"

"It's a police car, and there will be an ambulance along soon. Niko entered a nightclub and beat the snot out of a man who was seated at the bar."

"Leave the club. You don't need to become a part of a police investigation."

"I'm already across the street. After Niko left, I put my date in a cab and told her I would call her later. Then I called you."

"What was Niko driving?"

"I didn't get a good look at it, but it was red and might have been a Mercedes."

Henry waited for a response and heard nothing.

"Cody?"

"I'm here. I was thinking over what you've told me. Niko's actions would make sense if the man he beat was the same man who'd hurt the girl he was with, and it tells us two things."

"I know," Henry said. "It means that Niko has feelings for the girl and that he was willing to risk himself to get revenge on the man who hurt her."

"Yeah. He's impulsive, and foolishly so. That character flaw will someday be the death of him."

"Is that a prediction or the basis of a plan?"

"It's both."

"Hey Cody, I'm sorry I didn't react fast enough. If I had, I might have fulfilled the contract on Niko."

"No, Henry. From what you've told me, there was no time to act. Not with so many witnesses around. He'd also be looking out for anyone who followed him. Anyway, neither Niko nor his brother can be touched until someone is in place to kill the other man before they can get away. If you had killed Niko, Kirk Hyena would have been in the wind within an hour. Thanks to those monitoring bracelets they wear, they'll each know when the other one's heart stops beating."

"So, what's next?"

"I'm going to check out a hunch concerning Kirk Hyena. Sara will be with me, so you can have the day off."

"I'll take you up on that. Right now, I'm going to go see Bianca and check on her. She was upset by seeing Niko beat that other guy up."

"How big was the other man?"

"He was huge, and Niko took him apart like he was nothing."

"This trip definitely wasn't a waste of time, and maybe I'll learn more tomorrow. No matter what, when we return here, we'll be ready to go to work."

"On which contract?"

"That's the question, isn't it? Have a good night, Henry, and I'll see you tomorrow."

Cody ended the call and sat quietly. Sara had gathered what had happened from Cody's end of the conversation. Now she was staring at her husband.

"I can practically see the wheels spinning inside your head. What are you thinking about, the contracts?"

"Yeah. They're both challenging."

"And you want a crack at both, but you can't do that because of the distance and time limitations."

"Right. If I kill one brother, the other will take off before I can get to him."

"That's the greatest challenge. And I know you love a challenge."

"I was trying to figure out how to be in two places at once."

"Is that possible?"

"No."

Sara smiled. "If anyone can figure out how to do it, it would be you."

Cody tapped his finger against the side of his wineglass and sighed. He was torn on which target to take. Sometimes choice was not a good thing.

11

TUNNEL VISION

Niko had been surprised when Delilah returned to the bunker after dark. He had used the cameras' night vision and thermal capabilities to make certain she was alone before deactivating the land mines and other defenses. At his first sight of her battered face, he felt heartache. That was soon eclipsed by rage.

"Who did this to you?"

"His name is Hernando. If I don't bring him money, he will hurt me again... only worse. Oh Niko, please help me."

"This Hernando will be paid in full, Delilah. Where can I find him?"

Delilah had understood Niko's meaning and had shaken her head. "No. You can't hurt him."

Niko had grabbed her by the arms, then released her as he realized he had caused her pain by gripping her too tightly. After he calmed himself, he spoke to her in a soft voice.

"I want to know where Hernando is so I can make an arrangement with the man. I don't care if he wants to be paid every time we see each other. I have the money and I'll pay him what he wants. Now, where can I find him?"

"You won't hurt him?"

"We'll just talk."
"Do you promise?"
"Yes."

Delilah had named three places where Hernando might be. The first place, a bar, had been a bust, but when Delilah spotted Hernando's classic Thunderbird parked near the nightclub, Niko was certain he had tracked the man down and a change came over him. Delilah saw it, saw the rage building again, and had grabbed onto Niko's wrist to beg him not to hurt Hernando. Niko had shaken off her grip and pretended to calm himself again. That was the scene Henry had noticed as he was walking toward the nightclub. When Niko and Delilah went inside, Henry followed behind them with his date.

Once inside, Delilah had pointed Hernando out to Niko. With his target identified, Niko bolted toward Hernando and preceded to beat the man mercilessly.

~

DELILAH WAS SOBBING AND LOOKING TERRIFIED AS THEY WERE driving away from the nightclub. Niko told her to calm herself and promised her that Hernando would never hurt her again.

"Did you kill him?"

"He'll live, and he'll never forget that beating."

"We have to leave Juarez, Niko. Hernando is connected to the cartel. They'll send people to kill us. Oh God, why did you have to beat him?"

"I know he's connected to the cartel; if he wasn't, I would have killed him instead of beating him."

Delilah hugged herself. "Oh God, we have to run, hide somewhere, even your bunker won't be safe."

"It's all right, Delilah. No one from the cartel will harm us. They'll want money as compensation for Hernando, and for you, but they won't touch me. I'm higher up than a piece of shit like Hernando will ever be."

Delilah dried her eyes as she stared at Niko. "You are a member of the cartel?"

"I'm what you might call an associate. That bunker I'm staying in is theirs."

"But you said they'll want money. If you have the money, then why didn't you just pay Hernando for my time instead of beating him?"

"After what he did to you? You really think I would let anyone hurt you and get away with it? Hell no, I won't. And one more thing; you're done being a hooker."

"But I can't stop working. I need money for my little brother."

"Your mother can take care of him."

Delilah laughed bitterly. "She can't take care of herself; she's a drunk, Niko, and she's sick. I think it will just be me and my brother soon. He's only nine and I'm all he's got in the world. I have to take care of him, and I need money to do that."

"I'll give it to you."

"What, money?"

"As much as you need, but you're not hooking anymore."

"Why would you do that?"

Niko had left the streets and was on the highway. He pulled to the shoulder and placed the car in park. When he looked at Delilah, there was a sense of pleading in his gaze.

"Why do you come see me even when you aren't working?"

"I like you, Niko; you know that."

"Like me, is that all you feel for me, only like?"

Delilah broke eye contact as she said. "No, I feel more than that."

Niko took her hand. "I feel something for you too. Be my woman and I swear you'll never want for anything again."

"Your woman? I'm a whore. Why would you want someone like me?"

"That's in your past. Be faithful to me and it won't matter

what you've done before. I want to be with you, Delilah. I want you to be my woman."

Delilah grinned, then she pointed at her damaged face. "I'm a quick healer. I won't look like this for long."

Niko laughed. "You'll always be beautiful to me, baby. A few bruises don't change that."

Niko got the car moving again and was headed back to the bunker. Delilah noticed which direction they were traveling and asked Niko to take her home.

"If I'm not there, my brother will be all alone."

"Your mother is there, right?"

"She's useless, Niko."

"All right. Give me directions and I'll drop you off at home. But I want you to come see me first thing in the morning."

"I will, after I drop my brother at school, and I'll stay with you until I have to pick him up."

After Niko dropped Delilah at the entrance to her apartment house, he drove back to the bunker. He was wondering if he should admit to his brother that he was the one who assaulted the pimp Hernando or remain silent and hope the cartel wouldn't be able to identify him.

He decided to come clean and tell Kirk about the incident. He'd be furious, but Kirk needed to be prepared if the cartel phoned and asked for an explanation. It would also cost them a shitload of money to make things right.

"What the hell have you done?" Niko asked himself. After shaking his head in dismay, he grinned like a fool. Delilah was all his now, and they would be together forever. Niko still wasn't ready to admit to himself that he loved her, but it was true nevertheless, and even better, he was certain she loved him.

~

NIKO HAD LEFT THE BUNKER WITH DELILAH THROUGH ONE OF THE hidden tunnels. There were twenty-eight of them. They ranged in length from five hundred yards to ten thousand yards, and there were vehicles of one kind or another at the end of many of them. The shorter tunnels had floors and walls paved with concrete and had recessed lighting. The last two, the longest ones, which went on for miles, had dirt floors, were cramped enough that you had to crawl at times, and their roofs were supported by wooden beams. For light, one had to use a battery-powered lantern. Niko had taken one of the shortest tunnels. The car had been dead after sitting for so long, but there was a charging station to jump the battery.

Niko exited the tunnel with the use of a ramp that operated by a near-silent hydraulics system. When above ground, the ramp appeared to be a flat, wide, piece of rock. There were hidden cameras that let Niko see that no one was around before he used the ramp to drive out of the tunnel's exit.

Given the extensiveness of the bunker, Niko wondered how many millions had been spent to create it. If they'd had something like it back in their own country, they wouldn't have needed to flee.

∼

WHEN HE RETURNED TO THE AREA WHERE THE BUNKER WAS, HE kept a gun in his hand and looked about warily. When he was satisfied that there was no one about, he used a remote control to lower the ramp. It was a strange feeling to watch what looked like a solid surface sink into the ground. It was made stranger by the lack of noise and the glow of light coming from the tunnel.

He was careful to back the car slowly down the steep surface, and despite his desire to be free of it, it felt good to be back inside the bunker. He'd taken a hell of a risk venturing into the city while knowing there was a price on his head.

If Kirk thought I was a fool for running in the desert, he'll think I've lost my damn mind when he finds out about tonight, Niko thought.

After exiting the tunnel on his return to the bunker, Niko knew he was too keyed up to sleep, so he opened a bottle of beer and went online to play his favorite video game. He was joined by a player in the United States who went by the name of Rom Warrior.

Niko believed that Rom Warrior/Tim Jackson was there to play the game, and he was, but Tim was also gathering info for Tanner, and Niko's days were numbered.

12
THE PLANE TRUTH

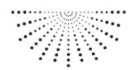

CODY HAD TOLD HENRY THAT NIKO'S FORAY INTO THE CITY HAD revealed two things about him, his impetuousness, and his feelings for Delilah. It wasn't until he had ended the call with Henry that Cody realized a third fact had been revealed—Niko had access to a vehicle.

It only made sense that he would, given the desolation of the bunker's surroundings. It would also be logical to assume that the vehicle was stored underground.

Early on in his apprenticeship with Spenser, Spenser had revealed a hidden space to Cody and Romeo that was in the Arizona desert. That space had been under a garage and was large enough to hold a pickup truck. The floor could be lowered to form a steep ramp using a system of pulleys. There had also been a ladder that could be used to exit the space in the event the pulley system failed. Niko's bunker must have something similar.

～

WHEN THEY RETURNED TO THEIR SUITE AFTER DINNER, CODY AND Sara went to bed early. Cody had been thinking about Kirk

Hyena. The man was a pilot. That might mean he had a plane nearby ready for his use if he were forced to flee the estate.

Since there was a small airfield located eight miles away from the estate, it seemed a good place to investigate. When Sara had learned of Cody's plans, she asked to come along.

"It could be dangerous."

"All the better," Sara said. "I've been bored now that we have everything at the ranch up and running so well. It's why I've decided to become a bounty hunter. Sneaking around in the middle of the night with you will be good practice for me."

"Bounty hunters sneak around in the middle of the night?"

"You know what I mean."

"Yeah, you're a thrill seeker."

"Hah! Then what does that make you?"

"I'm a highly trained assassin."

"And an adrenaline junkie too."

"You may have a point there," Cody said.

～

WHEN THREE A.M. CAME, THEY GOT DRESSED AND LEFT THE HOTEL to head for the airfield. There was a scent of smoke in the air, and they could hear sirens off in the distance. It wasn't unusual for something to be burning somewhere in a city of one and a half million people.

It was a clear night, and the stars were visible once they drew nearer to the desert. There was also enough of the moon showing to grant light to see by.

When they were in the area where the airfield was located, Cody slowed and shut off his headlights. If there was a guard on duty, he didn't want them wondering about the vehicle approaching. Given the flat terrain in the immediate region, the glow from the headlights could be seen from some distance away. The sound of the Jeep's engine would carry, so Cody went off-road and parked it in the shadow of a tree, an Afghan pine.

"We're on foot from here," he told Sara as they left the Jeep.

"When you said airfield, I thought it would be a small place, but I looked at it online and read that they have over twenty hangars. How will we know which plane belongs to Kirk Hyena?"

"I don't even know if he has a plane here, but if he does, I'm betting it's guarded day and night. Otherwise, someone could sabotage it and he'd kill himself the next time he took it up."

"If there is no guard, you could sabotage the plane yourself once you identified it."

"That's no good. I could never be sure that Hyena would be the only one on the plane when it went down."

"That's Tanner Tenet number two—Never kill the innocent. Right?"

"Yes. And sometimes that means I have to do things the hard way."

"Okay, then why are you so interested in the plane?"

"Because I may use it myself to escape once I've killed Kirk Hyena."

"So, you've decided? He's your target?"

"I haven't decided. I'm still exploring options. Both Romeo and Taran are pilots. If I hand the contract at the estate over to them, they would be able to use the plane too."

"That's the main reason you've taken this trip here, isn't it, to make things easier for whoever gets the second contract?"

"Yes. I want to give them as much information as I can, along with options. These are both tough contracts and there's no guarantee they'll survive the attempt at killing their target."

"That worries you, I can tell, but if Romeo or Taran accept the contract, it will be up to them to fulfill it. If something were to go wrong, you shouldn't feel guilty."

"I would feel partly responsible because I would be the one who asked them to take the contract, but nothing will go wrong, because I plan to also offer them a way to kill their man."

"You've never been in this position before, having to hand off a difficult contract to someone else."

"No. And I don't like it."

"Won't Henry be out on his own someday soon?"

"Yeah, but he'll be handling easier contracts in the beginning."

"Is that what you did?"

Cody smiled. "No, but I had Romeo watching my back and we worked as a team."

"You'll never need to worry about Henry because you're the one training him. If he's even half as good as you are, no one will stand a chance against him."

"He won't be half as good; someday he'll be better. That's the whole point of keeping the Tanner name alive."

"It may not be possible to be better than you are, Cody. And no amount of training can make someone something they're not."

"He'll be better, and he'll face different challenges than I did. Plus, he'll have a team behind him. Look how fast the world is changing, even I can't operate alone anymore. And I can't imagine what sort of world a Tanner Nine or Tanner Ten might have to deal with, but I do know one thing."

"What's that?"

"There will always be people who have committed acts that make them worthy of death, and there will be a Tanner to fulfill the contract on them."

~

THE ENTRANCE OF THE AIRFIELD AND THE AREA WHERE THE hangars were had a chain-link fence around them. There were also cameras. However, Cody was able to spot three gaps in the cameras coverage, so they picked one of those areas to climb over the fence. Cody was impressed when Sara scaled the fence almost as fast as he had. They were both dressed in dark colors and wore sneakers.

Each hangar had a bulb burning over its large doors but only two of them had a light on inside. They moved toward the glow of the nearest one and Cody peeked in through a corner of a window. He saw no one inside and was wondering if perhaps a light had been kept on by accident. Movement to his left changed his mind when he saw a black and white cat jump up onto a table. There was a food bowl there and the cat began eating.

He told Sara to take a look. She smiled and whispered, "Marian has asked about getting a cat. I told her she could have one when she was a little older."

"You had one when you were about her age, didn't you?"

"His name was Mr. Whiskers, and after that we had a cat named Fluffy."

"We had several cats around the ranch when I was growing up. My sisters named them all. The cats helped keep the mice population in check."

They moved on to the next building that had a light burning inside. It was Hangar Number Sixteen. Cody was unable to look inside through a window because there were curtains hanging up. He was able to see through the gap at the bottom of a rear door when he laid flat. There was a man seated at a table reading a book. He was armed and had on a guard's uniform.

Cody told Sara what he'd seen by whispering in her ear, then moved toward a vehicle that was parked nearby. He used a flashlight to check out the car's interior and saw a jacket. There was an emblem on the sleeve and words were written on it in Spanish—Alvarez Security Services.

"I think we've just located Kirk Hyena's plane. He's likely the only one who would have an armed guard on duty night and day."

Sara gasped as something brushed against her leg. It was the cat from the other hangar. Its owner had installed a pet door for its use. Sara reached down and petted it. Using her flashlight, she read the name tag on its collar.

"Gatita. That means kitty. How original."

Cody led the way over to the airfield's office. He disabled the simple alarm and picked the lock on the rear door.

"What are we looking for in here?" Sara asked.

"I need to know more about Hyena's plane. There should be a file here with information in it."

Cody was right, and he was glad when he saw a file cabinet. There had been the possibility that every record on hand was in a digital format. But no, the airfield kept hard copies of their info as well.

He found the file for Hangar Sixteen and was glad to see there was a photo of the plane inside and written down was its make, model, and registration number. There was also the name of its owner. That name wasn't listed as Kirk Hyena but was under the alias Kirk used to transact legitimate business; it was George Harper.

Cody took photos of the file. Later, he would send a copy of the file to Tim Jackson along with the name George Harper. Given Tim's expertise, Cody would soon know everything there was to learn about Kirk Hyena's alias.

He put everything back the way it was when he'd found it, locked the door, and reset the alarm. He and Sara were back in the car thirty minutes later and headed for their hotel.

"So, now you know he has a plane, and you know his alias. Is there anything else you need to do?"

"I'm going to return later and sit on the estate for a few hours. After that, we'll be done and can fly home tomorrow."

"This was a nice trip away from the ranch, but I miss my babies."

"I'm sure they miss you too. This is the first time we've both been away from them."

"Franny said they're taking it well, but that Marian keeps asking when we're coming back."

"I think she just wants the gift I promised her."

Sara laughed. "She's going to love that hat. She'll probably want to sleep with it on."

Cody reached over and gave Sara's hand a squeeze. "Thanks for coming along on this. I enjoyed your company."

"I could come with you to the estate too, if you'd like."

"No. Not only will it be boring, but it could also be dangerous."

"Dangerous how? I thought you would be watching it from miles away."

"I will be, but I might move in closer to test their security, or maybe I'll think of something else."

"Whatever you do, be careful."

"I will be. If I'm not careful I might tip off Hyena that he's being targeted. If he gets nervous, he may run to another hiding place, and I'll have to start over."

They returned to the hotel before five a.m., and after having an early breakfast together, Sara went back to sleep while Cody left to travel to the estate. This time he chose a spot that gave him a view of the fortress's rear. He was likely in for a boring day and knew it, but it also gave him time to think.

Inside the estate, Kirk Hyena was learning about his brother's latest impetuous activity.

13
THE CHOICE IS MADE

Kirk Hyena found out about Niko's beating of the pimp Hernando by watching a video of it on the news. A camera inside the nightclub had caught it and other videos captured on phones were being shown online.

Aroke had seen the video first and brought it to Kirk's attention. Kirk gestured at the screen. "I know I'm watching it with my own eyes, but please, tell me my brother is not that stupid."

Aroke moved closer to the television and pointed at a figure standing nearby. "That girl is the whore named Delilah. The man he's destroying is her pimp."

"This was all about the girl then? Niko must have lost his mind. The cartel will find out about this soon if they don't know already. I'll bet they'll want a fortune to make things right."

"That's a problem, but so is your brother. If he keeps leaving the bunker, sooner or later an assassin will get to him."

"Maybe I should send you to stay with him, to keep him from doing anything stupid."

"It wouldn't work. He wouldn't listen to me, and you wouldn't want me to use force against him."

Kirk grabbed his satellite phone. "Let's see what excuse he has to offer for his stupidity this time."

~

NIKO HAD STAYED UP UNTIL THE MIDDLE OF THE NIGHT PLAYING video games. When he was awoken by the sound of the satellite phone ringing, he wondered if Kirk was calling because he had found out what had happened the night before. He didn't have to wonder for long.

"Hello."

"Are you crazy? Why the hell did you beat up that pimp?"

"He hurt Delilah. You should see her face, Kirk."

"That's none of your business, Niko. The girl is his whore, his property, and they both belong to the cartel."

"Not anymore. Delilah is with me now. Pay the cartel whatever they want, but she's mine."

"Yours? What are you saying? You're going to be a pimp?"

"Delilah is no longer working for anyone. She's with me now; she's my woman."

"You're serious?"

"Yes. I want her, and she wants me too."

"She's a whore; all she wants is your money."

Niko had to calm himself before he spoke again.

"Don't call her a whore. Her name is Delilah."

"You've lost your mind. You do know that, yes?"

"I can't help how I feel."

"You've not only harmed our relationship with the cartel, but you've also risked your life by going into the city. What if this Delilah had been part of a plan to get you to leave the bunker? She would have led you right into a trap."

"She's not like that."

"But she could have been, Niko, and if she was, you'd be dead right now. Don't you understand that there's a contract out on us? You can't go running around like nothing's wrong or you'll wind up with a bullet in your head. You need to think before you act."

Niko sighed. "I hear what you're saying. But what would you have done if it had been your woman who'd had the shit beaten out of her?"

"I don't have a woman; I've learned they're nothing but trouble."

"You used to have a woman. I remember how much you were into that French girl, Elena."

"I was younger then, and foolish."

"You loved her; I know you did. Now, imagine if she came to you with her face all banged up by some guy."

"I didn't say there wasn't a reason to beat up the pimp, I just said it was stupid to do so. And expensive. Do you have any idea how much this is going to cost us? And that's assuming the cartel will be willing to settle for money."

"Of course, they'll want money. That's all they ever want. And remind them that I could have killed that pimp Hernando instead of messing him up bad."

"I want to meet this *woman* of yours when I travel to the bunker next month."

"You'll like her, Kirk."

"We'll see."

"And I'll stay inside the bunker from now on."

"No, you won't. You'll do whatever you feel like doing."

"I mean it. I'll stay inside."

"Goodbye, Niko. I have to get busy fixing this mess you've made for us."

The connection ended and Niko stared at the satellite phone. His brother was angry, but he'd get over it. After noticing what time it was, he rose from the bed with a smile on his face as he headed into the bathroom. Delilah would be at the bunker in less than an hour. As he showered, Niko sang a song about love.

The hours Cody spent watching the rear of the estate had resulted in him identifying what the outer buildings were used for. The largest one was obviously the barracks for the guards, and he'd observed them coming and going from it during a shift change.

A smaller building was a maintenance shop. The old man he and Henry had seen get out of the van must have been the estate's caretaker. Cody had seen him use a gray van to haul three broken chairs inside the shop. When he emerged an hour later, the wooden chairs were whole again, and he set them up on cardboard and applied stain to them.

The women from the van were the cooks and cleaners. One of them, a tall woman, brought out lunch to the old man and they talked and smoked outside after eating. The woman soon returned inside. While he was waiting for the stain on the chairs to dry, the old man went inside a glass building that was obviously a greenhouse and did some work in there.

Watching the man gave Cody an idea. When the van picked up the old man and the women later that day, Cody followed them from a distance.

~

When the van dropped the caretaker off in the city, he and the tall woman climbed into a box truck that had the name, Rangel Woodworking Designs written on its side in faded lettering. The truck was small and old, but it looked clean and polished. After dropping the woman off at a modest house, the old man waved goodbye and wound up at a bar.

Cody was about to go inside the bar when he spotted a home improvement store across the street. He went inside and bought a leather tool belt. It was the type a carpenter would use. He was carrying it when he entered the bar and found that the old man had settled on a stool near the end. Cody was wearing the glasses that changed his appearance and tamed his fierce gaze.

He sat two stools away from the old guy and placed the bag containing the tool belt on the floor. He made sure that a part of it was sticking up out of the bag.

The caretaker looked down at the bag and then up at Cody. When he spoke in his native Spanish, he revealed a raspy voice.

"You got the tools to fill that thing up, amigo?"

Cody looked down at the bag with a sour expression. "I've got the tools, and my old belt was ten times better than this new piece of crap, but the leather finally split in half, and now I've got to break in a new belt."

The old man nodded. "Yeah, they don't make them as tough as they used to. When I was your age, the tool belt I had belonged to my father. The thing must have been over thirty years old before I finally needed to replace it."

"Huh, my old belt had belonged to my father too, and yeah, the thing was worn-out, but it fit me like a second skin."

The old man went on to give his opinion about the best way to soften up the new belt. It included using rubbing alcohol and Vaseline, then letting the leather dry in the sun. During the conversation, Cody had moved over to take the stool beside the old guy and order more beer for them.

The man's name was Antonio. And up close, Cody could see that Antonio wasn't as old as he had thought. He guessed that he was maybe about sixty. By the time Antonio was on his fourth beer, Cody had him talking about the estate.

"It's a huge place, and you should see the men guarding it. They're all narcos who have probably killed many times."

"What's so valuable that so many men have to guard it?"

"There's a man living there who they say is a friend of the cartel's leader. I heard that someone wants him dead."

"Is it safe for you to be there?"

Antonio waved that off. "It's safe. There's a wall around it, and no one in their right mind would come near that place, not with all those killers around. If someone slipped past the guards, the dogs would get them."

Cody hadn't known there were guard dogs. That hadn't been a part of the information he'd received.

"Pet dogs?" he asked Antonio.

Antonio laughed. "Oh no, these are some kind of Pit Bull mixed breed. There are four of them and I think they each weigh as much as I do. My niece works there too, as a cook. If I didn't think it was safe, I wouldn't have her working there."

"You said the estate is huge, do you have a helper?"

"No, but the place is empty more often than not. When it's quiet again, I'll catch up on my work."

"How many rooms does it have?"

"Fourteen, along with a large kitchen and eight bathrooms."

"You must keep busy in a place that big."

"What kind of work do you do?"

"I do carpentry for a guy who fixes up run-down houses. Get this, he takes most of the money he makes and buys old stamps with it."

"Stamps? You mean the collectible kind?"

"Yeah."

"The guy living at the estate does the same thing. I had to replace a light fixture in the master bedroom, and I saw him looking at these old stamps. He held one up and told me it had cost more than I made in ten years. I wouldn't have given him a peso for the thing."

Cody changed the subject for a while by discussing what was on TV. It was a highlight reel of the best moments in soccer from the past season. During a commercial break Antonio removed a photo from his wallet and slid it over to Cody.

"Take a look at that."

It was a photo of a shop. The sign over the front door read: Rangel Custom Woodwork. There was a man standing in front of the shop. It was Antonio when he still had dark hair.

"This was your shop?"

"It was. It burnt down about twelve years ago. Madre de Dios but I loved that shop. I was my own boss and people paid me to create works of art for them. I'm just a handyman now, but at one time I was an artisan. I specialized in building custom tables, and I was making good money at it."

"Why didn't you open your shop again after the fire?"

"The insurance company denied my claim, the crooks. It took me a lot of years to save up enough to open that shop the first time. I was alone then, but now I have my niece and her little girl. Her husband was no good and ran out on her."

Antonio showed Cody three more photos. They were pictures of some of the custom tables he had built. They looked fantastic.

"Why don't you do work like this again, during your off hours?"

"I'm too damn tired these days. Things aren't so bad. I make good money, and no one bothers me. It could be worse."

Cody later brought the conversation back to Antonio's job. He did this while buying Antonio whiskey. By the time he'd left the bar, he knew that Kirk Hyena was spending most of his time in the master bedroom, which was on the third floor, and that there was a private elevator inside the room, along with a floor safe that weighed more than a ton. The safe wasn't part of the estate, but had been brought along when Kirk Hyena moved in. Antonio had also stated that the men guarding the estate were bored.

However, the most interesting thing Cody had learned was that Kirk Hyena was planning to leave the fortress during the upcoming holiday celebration of Our Lady of Guadalupe Day. Everyone was getting the time off, including the guards.

Antonio had no idea where Kirk Hyena would be going during the celebration, but Cody guessed that he might be visiting his brother inside the bunker. That meant that both targets could be in one place at the same time. Interesting.

And although it would be tempting to go after the targets at that time, the bunker would be next to impossible to get inside without being noticed. And once noticed, the Hyena brothers could use a tunnel to escape. The last thing Cody wanted was for the brothers to get away. If that happened, he might have to spend weeks or months tracking them down.

It would be better to let them spend time together and feel safe. Then, when they were confident that their defenses were too tough for an assassin to penetrate, it would be time to strike.

On his drive back to the hotel, Cody went over all he had learned during the trip. It was enough to fashion a plan with, or rather, two plans, one for the assassination of Kirk Hyena, and the other for the contract on Niko.

He was still conflicted about which target to go after himself but was leaning toward making Kirk Hyena his choice. Although, breeching the bunker would be a greater challenge.

Cody went out to dinner that night and found himself preoccupied by thoughts of what he would do when he returned to Juarez to fulfill a contract. He had learned from Nadia that Romeo was already committed and that he wouldn't be able to be in Mexico in the coming weeks. That meant that Taran would have to be contacted and offered the contract. Cody had faith that Taran would be successful no matter which target he gave him.

He had trouble going to sleep that night because his mind was pondering different scenarios that he could use. When they flew out in the morning, he was still undecided about what to do.

He put the matter from his mind after flying home and being greeted by his children. Marian loved her red sombrero and Lucas grinned as he slipped into the poncho.

Marian strapped on Lucas's toy guns and declared that she was a bandito. She giggled as she chased the dog, Lucky, around the living room while calling him the sheriff.

After taking Lucas for a ride on his pony, the children were put to bed and Cody settled in the office to once again look over the file Lawson had given him. While doing so, he received a text from Taran. Taran wouldn't be able to take a contract anytime soon because he was in Russia and would be there until January. That meant that Lawson would have to use a mixture of American and Mexican federal agents to capture and kill either Niko or Kirk. That was something Lawson had been hoping to avoid. Cody wasn't crazy about the idea either because it would mean he'd have to rely on people he didn't know to carry out their end of a coordinated attack.

After concluding that he needed to let his mind take a rest from the matter, he joined Sara and Franny in the living room and watched a movie about bank robbers.

Being tired from his lack of sleep the previous two days, he slept well and woke up late. He was tempted to go back inside his office and come up with a definitive plan for the Hyenas. Instead, Cody spent an hour helping Bobby Lincoln cut firewood, then went off for a long ride on his horse after lunch. It was while he was out riding that he came to a decision about what he would do, and he felt the tension leave him.

Upon returning to the house, he contacted Lawson and let him know of his decision, then he sat quietly and devised a plan to kill Kirk Hyena.

14

EXPERT HELP

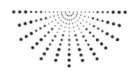

BACK IN MEXICO, KIRK HYENA WAS IN A FOUL MOOD. NIKO'S thrashing of the pimp, Hernando, was a bigger deal than Kirk had thought it would be. Hernando was the nephew of a higher up inside the cartel. That man wanted Niko's balls cut off, but he eventually settled for a large sum of money.

On top of that, more money had to be dished out to other people, and the fee for the use of the estate and the bunker had increased.

Altogether, Niko's gallantry in defending the honor of his hooker girlfriend had cost them nearly a million dollars. Buying Delilah from the cartel had been a hundred-thousand-dollar expense all on its own. A hundred thousand dollars. Niko could have rented Delilah every night for years and it wouldn't have cost that much. It left Kirk wishing that Hernando had beat the girl to death when he'd had the chance.

More bad news arrived when Kirk learned that the fighting in Almalia had increased because the people who'd ousted him from power had acquired new weapons. His forces had suffered losses. That meant the fighting would continue and there was no telling when he and Niko might be able to go home again.

As if those worries weren't enough, there had been talk about a joint task force of American and Mexican federal agents being formed to storm the bunker where Niko was staying. So far, it was only a rumor. What had been confirmed was that an elite assassin had been hired and was on his way to Mexico to kill a "High-value target." His contact within the cartel speculated that it might be Tanner himself. If that was true, Kirk feared for his brother's life. Niko's recklessness and lack of good sense might wind up getting him killed. If not by Tanner, then maybe by a Federale.

It's that damn girl, Kirk thought, meaning Delilah. Delilah had brought nothing but trouble into their lives and he had no doubt that she was using Niko because he had money. During their last conversation, Niko had mentioned bringing Delilah back to Almalia to live with him once they had regained control of the country. Kirk had said nothing in response but knew he would never let that happen. He'd see the girl dead first, and the idea of her death appealed to him greatly. If she were dead, Niko would mourn her, but he'd eventually forget her.

Of course, it would have to look like an accident or Niko wouldn't rest until he punished her killer. And it had to be done in such a way that it could never be tied back to him. That meant he couldn't use the cartel and would have to remain anonymous. His best option was to hire his own assassin using the internet. And it would be ideal if the assassin was someone who specialized in causing "accidents."

Kirk sighed. Hiring a hitter to kill Delilah would mean that the girl was costing him yet more money. But it would be worth it.

He'd let Niko have fun with the girl for a while and treat her well during his visit to the bunker. That way, Niko would never suspect he was behind her death when it happened.

With his mind made up. Kirk relaxed, went to the safe, and brought out his stamps. Since he was a boy, it always made him feel better when he spent time looking at them.

In Texas, Cody had come up with a plan to kill Kirk Hyena that would leave him avoiding having to make it past the estate's defenses and guards.

It was based on his earlier idea to use Kirk's passion for rare stamps against him, but Cody had refined it after talking to the caretaker, Antonio. The new plan should make Kirk eager enough that he would risk having a meeting without his army of protectors. Once that happened, his fate would be sealed.

Antonio had mentioned that the estate would be empty for two full days during the upcoming celebration of Our Lady of Guadalupe Day. He had also mentioned that there was a large safe that belonged to Kirk Hyena. It seemed logical to assume that Kirk Hyena would keep his rare stamps inside that safe. It was also reasonable to assume he might leave them there while he visited his brother inside the bunker. Although Cody had to admit there was an even chance that he might take the stamps with him. If that was the case, then Cody would have to contact Spenser and arrange to use the lure of the rare 2-cent Hawaiian Missionary stamp.

That might work and it might not. As valuable and uncommon as the stamp was, it was still only one stamp, and Kirk Hyena had no emotional attachment to it. As for his own collection, it seemed a certainty he would go to lengths to have it back once it was taken from him.

Being an assassin, Cody knew little about breaking into safes, but he did know someone who might have general knowledge about such things; it was his brother, Caleb. Caleb also went by the name of Stark and was a thief who stole from other thieves. Caleb had been adopted by an ex-Los Angeles cop named John Knox and had grown up on a farm in California. The money he took from the thieves he robbed went towards funding a charity Caleb ran, and which benefitted teens who were headed down the wrong path.

Caleb, along with his adoptive sister, Sadie, had helped turn lives around and kept dozens of teens from going down a track that would lead them to spending a life behind bars. Cody gave him a call and asked for his help.

∾

"Hey, big brother, it's good to hear from you."

"It's great to hear your voice too, but this isn't just a social call. I need your expertise."

Cody gave Caleb an overview of the situation. When Caleb asked what the type and model of the safe was, all Cody could tell him was what he had learned from the Mexican caretaker, Antonio, that the safe was huge and looked old.

"It would help if you had details. I'm no expert with safes, but I know two men who are. They were both safecrackers back in the old days. When they got out of prison, John Knox helped them by giving them jobs on the farm. They're both retired now, but they've forgotten more about safes than I'll ever know."

"Let me call you back tomorrow. I might have a way to get that information," Cody said.

∾

His next call was to Tim Jackson. Tim told him that he had been about to call him.

"You have news?"

"Yeah. I've hacked into Niko Hyena's satellite phone and have recorded a conversation between Niko and his brother. Other than their names, I couldn't make out heads or tails of it because they were speaking in what sounded like Arabic."

"It's not Arabic, but it's close. It's the language they speak back in Almalia."

"I can tell you that Kirk Hyena didn't sound happy. If I had to guess, I'd say they were arguing about something. Niko has also had conversations in English with a woman named Delilah. It sounds like she's his girlfriend. I'll send you those recordings, and any new ones that might come in."

"As usual, Tim, you've surpassed my expectations. I'm hoping you'll be able to help me with something else."

"Just name it," Tim said.

Cody asked Tim if there was any way he could find out more about the safe Kirk owned.

"You say he had it shipped there when he moved in?"

"Yeah."

"If I can find the name of the moving company he used, they might have some information about it in their system."

Cody recalled the name that was written on the side of the van that ferried Antonio and the other domestic workers to and from the estate.

"It's possible it's a company named Lopez Transport that is located in Juarez, Tim. Hyena might have used the name George Harper when he hired them."

"Lopez Transport and George Harper, okay, got it. I'll look into it and get back to you as soon as I can."

~

By noon the next day, Tim had come through. He had broken into Lopez Transport's computer files and found an account for George Harper.

"The file is in Spanish, and I had to do some translating, but I have to say that whoever does the paperwork at Lopez Transport is thorough. They had the safe listed by size, weight, and had written down the model number. I'd guess it was all for insurance purposes in case something went wrong during the move."

"Great work, Tim, thank you."

"No problem, and hey, enjoy Thanksgiving, Tanner, if I don't talk to you before then."

"You too, and say hello to Madison for me."

~

ONCE CALEB HAD THE SAFE'S MODEL NUMBER, HE WAS ABLE TO get advice from his contacts.

"They say it's a tough one to crack, Cody, and recommend that you use explosives."

"That might not be the best thing; the contents I'm after are delicate."

"My guys say you won't need a lot of it, just enough to blow apart the lock, oh, and you'll need to drill a hole first. I had them both write the instructions down and it looks like they agree with each other. Gregory, one of the guys, he says he could have blown the safe and been gone from the scene in less than five minutes. But remember, he's a pro."

"I appreciate the help, Caleb."

"You're welcome, and there's more."

"What is it?"

"What you're planning to do has been done before by a pair of guys in Southern California. I think they even plied their trade in Mexico a time or two. You could pretend to be them. The FBI called them the Ransom Bandits."

"Are they still operating?"

"No one has heard from them in almost two years. They either crossed the wrong people, went up on other charges, died, or retired."

"What's known about them?"

"They were believed to be American because the one who'd make contact with their victims had a thick southern accent."

"The Ransom Bandits? The name fits, and I think I'll use it. Kirk Hyena can think of me as being anything other than an assassin for my plan to work."

"I'd love to help you out in Mexico, but I'm too busy here."

"Are you sure you can't make it for Thanksgiving this year?"

"I'd like to, but we've got too much going on at the farm with the kids. I do plan to spend Christmas with you."

"We're thinking about heading to New York City after the new year starts. You're welcome to come there."

"That sounds like fun, but I couldn't be away from the farm that long."

"Too bad. I'd love to spend more time with you."

"I'll make it a point to be at the ranch during Christmas, and I'll bring my niece and nephew a ton of toys."

"They're already spoiled."

"Then a little more won't hurt. Goodbye, big brother, and be safe down there in Mexico."

∼

OVERALL, CODY'S PLAN WAS COMPLEX AND RELIED HEAVILY ON human nature. He was confident it would work, but if something went wrong, either Kirk or Niko could get away. There was also the problem of coordinating the two assassinations so that they took place around the same time. That had to happen.

To bring his scheme to life, Cody had contacted Duke in Manhattan and explained what he wanted. As usual, Duke knew someone who could supply what was needed for a price. Some of it would be shipped to Texas, while the rest would be ready and waiting for Cody by the time he returned to Mexico. But that was in the future and still weeks away. In the meantime, Cody was at home on his ranch and ready to celebrate the Thanksgiving holiday with his family.

He and Sara were also playing host to old friends.

15
GUESTS FOR DINNER

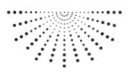

THANKSGIVING MORNING FOUND CODY AT AN AIRFIELD IN Brownsville, Texas. He had flown there to pick up the three guests that would be staying at the ranch for a few days. They were flying in on a private jet under assumed names. It was necessary to travel in such a manner to maintain their safety.

The man exited the jet first and looked around. He was dressed in a suit without a tie and was wearing mirrored sunglasses and a hat. When he spotted Cody, his posture grew less rigid as he relaxed. After sending Cody a wave of acknowledgement, he called to his fellow travelers who were still inside the jet. They were a woman and her young son.

After thanking the pilot of the jet, the man and woman walked over with their suitcases rolling along behind them and with a bag clutched in their other hands.

"Welcome to Texas," Cody said. The man was Joe Pullo. Pullo shook Cody's hand as Laurel came over and gave Cody a peck on the cheek. Their young son, Johnny, was smiling.

"Hi, Uncle Cody."

"Hey there, Johnny. Lucas is looking forward to seeing you again."

They climbed into Cody's plane with Pullo sitting up front in the cockpit. When Cody looked at him, he saw a worried expression.

"It's no jet, but this plane is just as safe if that's what you're concerned about, Joe."

"Hmm? Oh, no, I'm not worried about your piloting skills. No, I've got something else on my mind. We'll talk about it later."

"Is there trouble back in New York City?"

Joe sighed. "It's only a matter of time, isn't it? Someone's always looking to take my turf away."

"You know I'll help you if you need it."

"I do want your help, but just advice. I need a second opinion that I can trust before I decide what to do."

"What to do about what?"

"The future of the Giacconi Family. But we'll talk later, right now, I'm looking forward to chowing down on some good home cooking. You Texans eat turkey, right? Or did you barbecue a steer?"

"There's turkey, and beef, and fish too. Franny went all out this year and Sara helped. I'll be eating leftovers for a week."

Cody got the plane in the air and headed for the ranch. It was a mild day and there wasn't a cloud to be seen anywhere. When Cody looked back into the passenger compartment, he saw that Johnny was smiling as he looked out a window.

"Johnny's not afraid to fly, is he?"

Pullo laughed. "Nothing scares that kid. Last week, he climbed up onto the top of the china cabinet, took a leap, and grabbed ahold of the chandelier to swing from it. Laurel was scared to death when she saw him, but Johnny just laughed."

"He got that from your side; not much scares you either."

Pullo nodded. "I was that kind of kid too. If I'd thought it would be fun, I'd try it. That's why I broke my leg as a boy while jumping from roof to roof."

"How high up were you?"

"Three stories. I would have broken more than a leg if I

hadn't latched onto a fire escape for a moment on the way down. When the cast came off, I waited a few weeks to let my leg get strong and then jumped off the same roof and onto to one I missed the first time. I had to prove to myself I could do it."

"How old were you?"

"Nine."

They landed at the ranch and were greeted by Sara and Lucas, along with the dog, Lucky. The boys asked if they could walk to the ranch house instead of riding in a vehicle and were told that they could. They went running off with Lucky while laughing. Although Lucas was younger than Johnny, he wasn't much shorter because he was tall for his age. His long legs helped him to keep up with his older friend.

Laurel looked after them. "Will they be all right?"

"Yes," Sara said. "Lucas knows the way well. They'll probably reach the ranch only a minute or so after we do by cutting across the fields." After speaking, Sara gave Laurel a hug. "It's good to have you here."

Laurel hugged her back. "It's good to be here."

∼

HENRY AND HIS GRANDMOTHER, LAURA, WERE THE OTHER GUESTS at the table. Cody had introduced them while everyone had been in the living room with the children. When Laura realized who Pullo was she stared at him with an open mouth before speaking.

"Um... I... um, it's nice to meet you, Mr. Pullo."

"Call me Joe, and you're Laura, yeah?"

"Yes."

"It's a pleasure to meet you, and I've heard a lot about your grandson here."

"Henry is quite a boy, or I should say man. He's grown up so fast that it makes me feel old."

Pullo looked Laura over. She was past fifty, but she had kept her figure and didn't look her age. "You don't look old to me."

"Don't you flirt with her," Laurel called over from the sofa; she had a smile on her face.

Franny helped to serve dinner but wasn't staying to eat. She had an invitation to dine at Caroline Lang's home with Caroline's father, Crash, the man she was seeing. She remained at the house long enough to hear the compliments her cooking received. As she left, she carried a sweet potato pie and a strawberry shortcake with her, because she had volunteered to bring dessert to Caroline's home. She'd made double of everything, so Cody and his guests could also enjoy her baking.

An hour after starting the feast everyone was full and was sipping on coffee or soda. Later, Laurel and Laura told Sara that they would help her with the dishes and the kids were placed in the living room to watch a cartoon movie about talking insects.

Henry had a date with a girl he'd met at the diner, and they were going to take in a movie. He told his grandmother he would see her in the morning and left.

Cody and Joe had carried the serving trays into the kitchen before being shooed away by their wives. They settled in the office where they sipped on wine while sitting in a pair of leather wing chairs.

"That kid Henry is going to be a Tanner someday?"

"That's the plan."

Joe shook his head. "Talk about having big shoes to fill. You're going to be a tough act to follow, Tanner... I mean, Cody."

"Henry has what it takes; he'll do fine."

Joe asked about the ranch and the Parker Training Center. Cody answered his questions while wondering what was on his mind. Whatever it was, he wasn't eager to talk about it, but Cody knew his friend would get around to discussing it eventually. He was right, and after getting up and pacing for a moment, Pullo spoke.

"If things don't change, the Giacconi Family is doomed."

Cody poured more wine. "What's your plan to fix that?"

Pullo released a heavy sigh. "I'll have to do something I'd never thought I'd do."

"To avoid the end of the Giacconi Family?"

"Yeah."

"And that means what?"

Pullo collapsed into his seat and drained his wine glass. "It means leaving the Mafia."

16

THE INEVITABLE AND THE UNTHINKABLE

JOE PULLO WAS SHOWING A SIDE OF HIMSELF THAT CODY HAD never seen. Pullo looked like a man caught in a bear trap who was considering hacking off his foot to get free.

"Joe, you thinking about leaving the Mafia is like the pope considering becoming an atheist. What's happened to bring this on?"

"Do you remember that conversation we had about a year ago inside the office building during the war with the Primeros?"

"Yeah," Cody said, and thought back over what had been discussed.

∽

A STREET GANG WITH CHAPTERS ACROSS THE COUNTRY WAS making a bid to take over New York City. They were called the Primeros. Thanks to Tanner, they'd been dealt a hard blow, but there was no doubt that the war would continue.

Tanner had entered the office building owned by the Giacconis by using a secret tunnel that connected the building to a pizza parlor that was farther down the block. Pullo had met him, and they were taking an elevator up to the conference room.

When the elevator stopped moving, the doors opened to reveal the inside of a supply closet. There was a space between stacks of copy paper that was wide enough to walk through in single file. Pullo stepped off first with Tanner following. After the elevator doors closed behind him, Tanner looked back to see that they had blended into the wall. The closet led to an empty office, then to a carpeted corridor. As they passed a window, Tanner saw that they were on the third floor of the office building.

"That Italian thing gets in the way sometimes, doesn't it?"

Pullo considered the question, then nodded. "I'm not as strict with it as old Sam Giacconi had been. If I was, Finn and Rico wouldn't be here."

"But they'll never be made members either, right?"

"It's not allowed. They're considered 'associates.'"

"That's a problem your enemies don't have. The Primeros have gotten so huge because they accept anyone no matter their race, and also women. If they continue to get bigger while you stay the same, you'll never beat them in the long run."

Pullo had stopped walking and stared at Tanner. There was anger showing in his eyes.

"Don't you think I know that? But what can I do? We're the Mafia, damn it, and that means we're Italians."

"But it doesn't have to; Finn and Rico prove that."

"The Commission in Chicago would have to give the okay for me to start recruiting non-Italians in huge numbers. I don't see them doing that. Those guys are all old-school."

"They also don't have anywhere near the power they once had, and it's the Primeros that run Chicago these days. The same thing will happen here if you don't make changes."

"What are you, an expert on the Mafia now?"

"No. I just don't want to see you get killed someday, Joe. And

I don't see the Primeros backing off just because of what happened tonight."

∼

"I've given that conversation a lot of thought and you were right. If we keep sticking to the Italian only thing, we'll be lucky to make it another ten years. Hell, the Mafia isn't a third of what it was when I was born, and it was nothing then compared to what it had been back in Sam's day. I don't see the Giacconi Family surviving unless we make some serious changes."

"Such as recruiting people who aren't Italian?"

"Yeah. And I'll tell you, that doesn't bother me. Look at Finn Kelly. No one is better at running things than he is and most people like him and would go out of their way to do what he says. But if I had to step down and name a successor, I couldn't pick him to lead the family because he's not Italian. Sammy is the future of the Family, don't get me wrong, but he's not ready to take over yet. Right now, Finn would be a better choice, but Sammy is Italian, and Finn isn't."

"Okay, so you start recruiting people who aren't Italian. How will your own people feel about that?"

Joe made a face. "They'll hate it. I'll also have Jerry Magdalena and the other mob commissioners looking to replace me."

"Would that mean you'd have to go to war with the other families?"

"It might. And that's the last thing I want. If we start killing each other, it will only make us weaker and ripe for a group like the Primeros to come in and take over."

"I thought they were busy fighting their own war against another gang."

"They are, but it looks like peace could be right around the corner there. Once things settle down, they may turn their attention back on New York. They outnumber us; if they keep coming, there's no way we'll win that war."

"Tyrese and the Boulevard Bloods would fight alongside you."

Joe smiled. "They would. Tyrese has become a good friend and he runs the Bloods like a well-oiled machine. If they were all Italian, I would have already brought them into the Family."

"But they're not Italian, they're black, and Jerry Magdalena and the mob commissioners would put a hit out on you if you ever tried that."

Joe nodded. "Yeah. You see the problem? If I do nothing, it's just a matter of time before the mob is run out of New York City. If I make a move to prevent that, my own people will take me down. But what am I supposed to do, sit back and watch it all go away?"

"It's a dilemma, but there is a third option."

Pullo had been staring at the floor. He raised his head with a hopeful expression after Tanner announced there might be another alternative.

"What third option?"

"Walk away. Name a successor other than Sammy and take him and your family somewhere and start a new life. These young gangs are hungry for new territory and don't respect boundaries. They would kill Laurel and Johnny as soon as they would kill you. They've been threatened before and it could happen again. Walk away, Joe. Just walk away and let nature take its course. The Mafia came about because it was bigger and stronger than the gangs it replaced. The same thing will happen to the Mafia someday, and it's already happened in other cities. Get out while you still can."

Pullo was shaking his head. "I can't do that. I know it's the smart move, but I can't walk away without having done something first. And Sammy would never come with us. His last name is Giacconi. He'd stay and fight for that turf until they killed him."

"Okay, what's your plan?"

Pullo chuckled, but there was no sound of humor in it. "I don't have a plan yet. I just keep gnawing on this like a dog with a bone."

"When you decide what to do, let me know if I can help."

"Cody, no, Tanner, you're the only reason the Giacconi Family is still around. We would have been destroyed years ago without your help. And I can't keep asking you to fight our battles for us. We have to find a way to survive on our own."

"I'll still help if you need me."

"I know, buddy, and I'm grateful as all hell, believe me. Anyway, enough of my problems, what's going on with you?"

Cody went on to tell Joe about the Hyena brothers.

"Two hits at the same time. That's tough to do. It doubles the chances that something can go wrong."

"Yeah, but I think the plan I have in place will work if everyone does their part."

"Good luck with that. And when are you coming back to New York?"

"Right after New Year's Day, and we'll spend a few weeks there."

"Great. The city ain't the same without you."

They left the office and rejoined their families in the living room. Marian was seated on Sara's lap and was wearing her red sombrero. She had rarely taken it off since receiving the present. Johnny and Lucas were on the floor and looking up at the TV. The Wizard of Oz was playing, and the children were mesmerized by it, as children had been for more than eight decades.

There was eggnog in a glass carafe sitting on the coffee table with matching crystal glasses. Cody poured some and settled in beside Sara to watch the movie. When he looked over at Pullo, he saw that his friend appeared more peaceful than he had seemed earlier. Perhaps talking out his problem had made him feel better.

But it was still a problem, and an inevitability. Someday, there would come a war to New York that the Giacconi Family wouldn't win. When that day came, Cody would do everything in his power to see that his friend survived.

For now, he would sip on eggnog, enjoy the Thanksgiving holiday, and deal with that future when it arrived.

17
BOOM!

By the time Sunday rolled around, Joe Pullo had been on a horse three times and was getting the hang of it. Laurel had grown up riding a horse and loved it, and Johnny Pullo did well on a pony.

When it was time for the Pullo family to head back home on Monday morning, Cody flew them to the airfield in Brownsville, Texas, where they would again board a jet. Joe told Cody that it had helped to talk things out with him.

"I still don't know what I'm going to do. Maybe I'll speak to some of the other bosses and see where their heads are at. I can't be the only one thinking this way."

"You're probably right, but if you talk about it, I'm sure word will get back to the commission in Chicago."

"Oh yeah, but that would happen anyway." Pullo offered his hand. "You've got a good life here, buddy. I'm a city boy at heart, but I can understand why you like the ranch so much."

"You're welcome here anytime, and I'll see you soon in New York."

"Do that."

Cody stayed and watched the jet take off, then headed back home.

~

A PART OF THE ORDER CODY HAD PLACED WITH DUKE CAME IN during the first week of December. They were reproductions of the locking mechanism that would be found on Kirk Hyena's safe. That lock was the combination type and was numbered 0 through 99. A seasoned professional safecracker might have the tools and expertise to figure out the correct combination and open the safe without damaging it. As a Tanner, Cody had a myriad of skills and talents, cracking safes wasn't one of them, so he would need to destroy the lock.

Cody would get one chance to break into the safe, but he now had four chances to practice doing so. The locks were encased in thick metal and attached to stands that had weighted bottoms to make them stable. The poles on the stands were adjustable; when they were in the lowered position, the whole thing was two feet high but four feet when extended. They each weighed eighty-seven pounds.

Cody had plastic explosive on hand and would use it on the locks. But first, he needed to find a quiet spot where he could practice.

~

HENRY JOINED CODY AND THEY DROVE FOR ABOUT HALF AN HOUR until they reached a desolate area. From there, Cody went off-road and traveled three miles to park behind a hill. A search with binoculars showed that there was no one else around, so they got to work.

"Are these locks exactly the same as the one on the safe, Cody?"

"They should be. Duke has never let me down yet."

"How do you want to do this?"

"We have to drill a hole first, then we'll use a little of the explosive on the first of the locks and see what happens. From there, we'll fine-tune it."

They removed the first lock from the bed of the pickup and adjusted its stand until it was about three and a half feet off the ground. Drilling the hole took over a minute and it was an effort to hold the cordless drill steady. The plastic explosive was like clay and would fill the hole and adhere to the lock's surface. With the substance being pliable, Cody was able to shape any excess around the lock.

After he'd fed the explosive inside the hole made for it, he inserted an electronic fuse. Then, he and Henry took cover at the side of the hill. When Cody sent a signal to the fuse, the sound of the explosion seemed mild. When they checked the lock, they saw that it had been damaged, but the lock was holding fast.

Henry was frowning. "Why don't we use a bigger drill bit and double the amount of explosive we used for the next one. That should do it."

Cody was already cutting a large piece off the block of C-4 he had. "I'm going to use four times as much and drill a wider hole."

"That should wreck it for sure."

"I think so, and if not, we'll know these things are tougher than they look."

The first lock went back into the pickup and a new lock came out. They had to wait for a small plane to pass overhead until they could try again. While waiting, Cody checked the surrounding landscape with the binoculars. He saw no one.

The next explosion was thunderous. When they came out from cover, they saw that the lock had been obliterated along with the pole it had been on.

Henry laughed. "Whoa, that would have blown the door off the safe."

"Yeah," Cody said. "And also destroy the stamps. We'll try an amount of C-4 that's somewhere in the middle of the first two."

Again, they checked to make sure that they were still alone before proceeding with the third attempt. When it went off, it was loud, but not deafening, at least, not out in the open air.

The lock was broken and the metal around it seared from heat. After inspecting the lock, Cody thought the damage wasn't that great. Had the lock been a little stronger it might have held.

"Okay, we've one left. Let's give it a little more of the explosive than last time."

They did that, and the lock had a mangled appearance, while the steel around it was singed but not warped.

Cody was pleased by what he was seeing. "I think we know how much to use now. Let's hope that Kirk Hyena leaves the stamps inside the safe."

"I think he will," Henry said. "Why go to all the trouble and expense of bringing the safe to the estate if you're just going to carry the stamps around with you?"

"That's what I think, but you never know what someone else might do."

"I know what he's going to do. He's going to die. If not one way, then another."

"And why is that?" Cody asked.

"Because you're a Tanner, and a Tanner never fails."

"That's right, Henry. It's what makes us the best, and you'll carry on that tradition someday."

∼

SARA ASKED IF SHE COULD RETURN TO MEXICO WITH CODY. SHE had enjoyed her middle of the night trip to the airfield and wanted to help if she could.

"This won't be the relaxed trip we had last time."

"I know. This time it's the real thing. I'm not expecting dinner and dancing, but I would like to help if I could."

Cody thought about it for a moment, then he nodded. "There

is something you could do. It might lead to nothing, but I'd like you to follow someone."

"I'm good at that. Who would you like me to follow?"

"It concerns Niko Hyena and the other assassination. You can be my eyes there since most of the time I'll be tied up and miles away dealing with Kirk Hyena."

"Do you think something will derail the second assassination?"

"No. It should go off smoothly when the time comes, but Niko has proven to be unpredictable. If he does something unexpected, you'll be there to see it."

"It sounds boring."

"It will be, but you did ask if you could help, and Henry will take turns with you."

"I'm not complaining; boredom is just a part of surveillance. When do we leave?"

"We've got another week or so before we return to Juarez, but I want to be there when Kirk makes his trip to the bunker to visit his brother."

"In case they get careless?"

"Yeah. If that happens, Henry and I will put them both down with sniper rifles."

"I want a rifle too."

"You'll have one, along with a bulletproof vest, night vision equipment, and anything else that will help keep you safe. Surveillance or not, you may face danger, Sara."

"I can handle myself."

"Tell me about it," Cody said, and Sara laughed.

18

CARAVAN

They were back in Mexico eleven days later. They were positioned near the estate when Kirk was to make his trip to the bunker.

Tanner was there with Henry. And it was Tanner this time and not Cody. He wasn't there to gather info but to fulfill a contract, and that made it all business.

Tanner wasn't surprised when the bulletproof limo arrived, but he was proven wrong when Kirk Hyena prepared to leave the estate's walls with every one of his fifty protectors surrounding him. They were a caravan of cars and pickup trucks and must have had enough firepower to slay a regiment. Getting everyone organized and ready to move was taking time. The narcos weren't disciplined soldiers but thugs, having them work as a team took effort.

Given that they were part of a cartel, they didn't have to worry about a cop pulling them over on their trip to the bunker. It wouldn't be a surprise if a paid-off cop escorted them there.

Through the lens of the zoom camera Tanner had made out what looked like several handheld grenade launchers. Most of the men had rifles and they all had sidearms. If they were attacked en route by anything less than a force of equal size and strength, they would either win or cost their foes dearly.

Tanner would be the exception to that rule had he turned his mind toward achieving that aim. He had not. He wasn't going to depend on overcoming the odds this time, as he had on other occasions. On this outing he was using guile and relying on human nature.

He would let Kirk reach his destination and have his visit with his brother. The man must feel that he was risking his life to travel, otherwise he wouldn't be doing so with half a hundred men protecting him. When he made the trip to and from the bunker without incident, he would be feeling more confidence and might even relax his guard. That was exactly what Tanner wanted him to do, and it was what was needed for his plan to work.

Tanner lowered his camera and tapped Henry on his arm. "Let's go. We need to be in position before they get there."

Henry nodded in understanding, and they left the hill and headed toward the vehicles they were using. This time it was a pair of gray Range Rovers. They climbed into the vehicles and headed toward the bunker, where Sara was already keeping watch.

∼

SARA STARTLED WHEN SHE HEARD THE CRUNCH OF FOOTSTEPS approaching her. It wasn't the sand behind her that crunched, no, the sound came from the sheets of aluminum foil she had buried in the sand around her.

"It's me, Sara," Tanner said. When he crested the hill behind her, Sara grinned at him.

"That trick with the foil works great as an early warning system."

"You can thank Tanner Two for that idea," Tanner said.

After kissing in greeting, Sara asked him where Henry was.

"I've got him keeping an eye on the highway. When Kirk Hyena's caravan gets here, I'm betting he won't drive up to the entrance to the bunker. It would be smarter for him to drive his bulletproof limo down into one of the tunnels. That way, if they're attacked, they'll be able to leave in the armored limo."

"And then you'll also know where one of the tunnels lets out."

"Yeah. And if Kirk and Niko get stupid and stick their heads up together, Henry will take them both out with a sniper rifle. That would sure save us a lot of time and trouble, but I don't expect it will happen."

Sara reported that she had watched Delilah arrive at the bunker two hours earlier. Delilah's scooter was parked where it had been the last time Tanner had seen her visit.

"She's an extremely good-looking girl," Sara said. "I can see why Niko Hyena fell for her."

"Kirk Hyena doesn't feel the same way. He thinks his brother is a fool for getting involved with her. Niko's beating up of her pimp also wound up costing them a lot of money. That's one reason you're here."

"What do you mean?" Sara said.

"If the brothers have an argument about her, Kirk might do something impulsive, like leaving the bunker without his men around him and returning to the estate before I can break into the safe."

"If he didn't have his guards, you and Henry could kill him before he reached the safety of the estate."

"No, Henry and I would have to let him return to his fortress. While we could attack the limo and kill Kirk, we'd still have no way to kill Niko. Unless the two of them show themselves out in the open together, we'll have to stick with the plan that's in place."

"When are you going after the stamps?"

"Tomorrow night. The estate will be deserted by then and the guards will be in the city celebrating. If any remain behind, Henry and I will take care of them."

"You mean kill them."

Tanner shook his head. "I won't be killing anyone. I need Kirk Hyena to believe we're thieves, not assassins. If we come across a guard, we'll knock him out with gas. I've got several canisters of it, thanks to Duke."

"Be careful. I'm sure the guards will be trying to kill you."

"I doubt there will be anyone around. If what I learned from the caretaker, Antonio, is right, everyone will be in the city during the celebration. The estate will be protected only by its electronic defenses."

"How are you going to get past those?"

"With help from Tim Jackson. He says he can hack into the computers of the security company Hyena uses. We'll set off every alarm and motion detector, but Tim will keep a notification from being sent out."

"And what if the stamps aren't in the safe?"

"Then it's on to Plan B and I'll have to ask for help from Spenser's client."

"Kirk Hyena might think it strange that a valuable and rare stamp suddenly becomes available right after someone made an attempt to steal his own collection."

"He might, but he'll also be tempted to acquire it."

"Is there a Plan C?"

"Yeah. In Plan C, I make it inside the estate, past the guards, and kill Kirk."

"How many guards are there again?"

"The number I was given by Lawson was fifty, and Henry and I have seen dozens of them."

Sara grimaced. "Let's hope the first plan works."

"It would be best," Tanner said.

A CALL CAME IN ON THE SATELLITE PHONE TEN MINUTES LATER. It was Henry telling Tanner that Kirk's caravan had left the highway and was headed for the bunker.

"Follow them, but stay back at least a mile."

"I may lose them if I stay back that far."

"You won't lose them; not with the amount of dust and sand they'll kick up. Once you have an idea where they'll be, call me and I'll come join you. If by some fluke of luck, you get the chance to kill them both, take it, then get the hell out of there. My guess is that you'll never see either one of them because that limo will be headed into a tunnel or some other hidden entrance."

"Understood," Henry said.

"Should I still keep watch here?" Sara asked.

"No. Head back to your vehicle and wait for the girl to leave, then follow her. She may have moved since the last time we were here, or she could be up to something and will meet with someone."

"You think so?"

"No. But it's best not to assume she's harmless. By intention or not she's gone from being a prostitute to hooking up with a wealthy man who freed her from her pimp. She's likely had good luck but it's also possible she maneuvered things to work out that way."

"That would make her a gold digger."

"And mark her as being conniving. A woman like that might get an idea to cash in on the contract placed on the brothers. If so, she's in a unique position to kill them both. She could poison their food, or maybe kill them in their sleep."

"And rob you of fulfilling the contract on Kirk Hyena."

"Yeah. That can't happen. Follow her, then let me know what you think of her."

"Okay."

A cloud of dust became visible in the distance and was about four miles away. After a minute, the dust subsided.

Tanner pointed at it. "I'll bet you that's Kirk's caravan. It's hard to keep a low profile in the desert when you're traveling with so many vehicles. Given how far away it is from the bunker's entrance, at least one of the tunnels goes on for miles."

Henry confirmed that when he called in. "I won't be using the rifle even if I get the chance. I had to stay back over a mile because some of the guards set up a wide perimeter. I was able to use the camera to see that the limo is no longer in sight. It must have driven down inside a tunnel or something."

"Stay away from that area even if the guards leave. There might be land mines around the tunnel's entrance."

"More land mines? This bunker is no joke."

"It's not, which is what makes it a challenge. Keep your head on a swivel, Henry, and I'll join you soon."

Tanner went with Sara to her vehicle, which was a white Jeep. After instructing her on how to use a device that he had placed in the glove box, they shared a kiss and then parted. By the time he reached Henry's position, the guards were leaving the area, and eager to start their time off for the celebration.

Henry pointed out the area where he'd last seen the limousine. "There must be an entrance somewhere over there, and I guess the opening is wide enough to drive into."

Tanner stared at the spot. "Both targets are here now. It's too bad we don't have a way in there."

"I thought of a way to get in, but it's not one we'd ever use."

Tanner gave Henry a sideways look. "You're talking about the girl?"

"Yeah. We know Niko would risk himself for her. If she were threatened, he might be angry enough to confront us or maybe even sacrifice himself for her." Henry held up a hand. "I'm not saying it's something I'd do, but I couldn't help but consider it as an option."

"I get you. The thought crossed my mind too, but she's an innocent as far as we know, and so she's off-limits. If we find out different about her, then yeah, she might be of use."

"What's next on the schedule?"

"We'll need a truck so we can pick up the crate Duke has sent. Once we open it, we can spend the rest of the day going over the contents and getting things ready. Tomorrow, during the day, we'll keep watch here while Sara follows the girl, Delilah, around."

"Then tomorrow night we break into the estate?"

"Yeah, and that will start the ball rolling."

"Why will Sara be keeping watch on Delilah?"

"Because I don't know much about her. I assume she's an innocent, but she might be more than she seems."

Henry smiled. "I see why you say I won't be working alone when I'm a Tanner. Contracts like this one are too complicated for one person. If your friend, Tim, wasn't helping us, along with Caleb, we would never have a chance to break into the safe."

"The world is getting more complicated. By the time you're my age, it may be unrecognizable in some ways. And yeah, you'll need a team behind you, and you'll have it. I'll make sure of that."

Tanner checked his watch. "Let's get going. We've a lot to do before tomorrow night."

They left the region around the bunker, as inside, Kirk Hyena was getting his first look at Delilah.

19

A HEART OF GOLD

Kirk smiled at Delilah and offered her his hand in greeting, as they met in the living room area inside the bunker. Kirk appeared genial on the outside, but he felt nothing but disdain for Delilah. However, Kirk was wise enough to know that revealing his true feelings in front of his brother would be a mistake. It was prudent to appear accepting of the girl.

Delilah sent Kirk a shy smile in return and looked nervous. Standing behind Kirk was Aroke. He knew Kirk's true opinion about Delilah and shared it. The girl was nothing but a whore looking to latch onto Niko for his money. Aroke didn't smile at Delilah; his gaze was blank. He was there as a lone security guard while the brothers spent time together. If he were to view Delilah as a threat to his employers' lives, he'd shoot her.

Niko draped an arm over Delilah's shoulders. "Is she beautiful or what?"

"She's very lovely, and she makes you happy. That's all that matters," Kirk said.

Niko grinned at him and placed his free arm around Kirk to hug him. The gesture pulled Kirk closer to Delilah and Kirk forced himself to keep a smile on his face.

When Aroke was introduced to Delilah the stoic bodyguard

sent her a nod. Delilah smiled at him, but the smile faltered when she looked into his cold eyes.

Aroke excused himself and said he wanted to roam the tunnels of the bunker to do an inspection. Kirk told him that was a good idea and took a seat on a sofa.

Niko made drinks, whiskey on ice, and handed one to Kirk. Delilah didn't drink liquor, not after seeing what alcoholism had done to her mother, so she was having a soda. She and Niko sat on a love seat that was positioned across from Kirk with a coffee table between them. It was Niko who broke the awkward silence.

"Did you have any problems on the trip here?"

"No. If someone was following me, they would have to be insane to attack while the guards were protecting me."

"Do you really think Tanner is after us?"

Kirk nodded his head toward Delilah. "Maybe we shouldn't talk about this in front of your young lady."

"Delilah knows everything. And when we're finally able to return to Almalia, she's coming with us; her and her brother."

"A brother?"

"My brother is named Tomás," Delilah said. "He's nine years old and is a good boy. He won't be any trouble and I'll take care of him."

Kirk was thinking that his own little brother was causing him nothing but trouble lately. He sent Delilah a smile and a nod. Niko's plans didn't matter because they would never take place. There was no way in hell Kirk would let Delilah set foot in his country, even if he had to kill her.

∽

DELILAH LEFT THE BUNKER AN HOUR LATER SO THE BROTHERS could have some time alone. Sara was two miles away and tucked out of view behind a sand dune. She heard Delilah's scooter before she saw it, then followed her into Juarez. When

Sara saw Delilah's scooter kick up sand while going over a narrow ridge that was set high above a rocky ravine, she slowed her speed to keep from raising a dust cloud of her own. If Delilah were to notice it, she might realize she was being followed. The ridge's sandy surface was a tight fit for the Jeep and didn't allow much room for error. If a driver were careless, they might wind up going over the edge. It likely wasn't a problem, since it wasn't part of a road, but rather a shortcut to reach one.

After entering the city, Delilah stopped at a supermarket. Sara had trailed behind her into the store and saw Delilah buy fresh carrots, potatoes, and then a pound of cubed beef, along with other items. It appeared to Sara that the girl was gathering ingredients for a stew. There was also a loaf of fresh baked bread.

As had happened on the day that Henry had followed her, Delilah had then driven to the apartment house where she lived with her mother and brother. It was on a well-traveled street and had a small courtyard area in front of it. In years past, the building had probably demanded high rent, but it was currently in sad shape and in need of maintenance. As usual, Tomás was outside in the courtyard playing soccer, but he ran over to his sister when he spotted her.

Sara watched as Delilah hugged her brother and kissed him on the top of his head. Their resemblance was obvious, and she assumed they were siblings.

She parked the Jeep and walked to a restaurant that was three doors down and across the street. After taking a seat at a table that gave her a view of Delilah's scooter, she sipped on coffee and kept watch.

An hour later, Sara returned to her car and waited some more. When Delilah did reappear, it was only to call out a third-floor window to her brother. She was telling him it was time to eat. Tomás said goodbye to his friends and ran inside the building.

When it was dark and the courtyard was empty, Sara left her car and walked over to Delilah's scooter. She was placing a tracking device on it that had a magnetic backing, as Tanner had instructed her to do. He had placed one in every vehicle in case the need arose to keep track of someone. Not only would the device make it easier for Sara to follow Delilah without being seen, but the app it came with would keep track of her movements while Sara was asleep or otherwise occupied. Having purchased them in Mexico, all the wording was written in Spanish. Not that it mattered much when the target you were following appeared as a dot moving across a map on your phone screen.

Once she returned to her vehicle, Sara gave it another hour to see if Delilah was going out after eating. When nothing happened, Sara drove off toward the hotel she was staying in. The following morning, she would begin her surveillance again.

~

Tanner arrived back at their suite as Sara was leaving the bathroom after having showered. He and Henry had spent most of the day going over the supplies Duke had sent him. Those supplies included three mechanical devices that needed to be tested before use. All three had worked well and had been refilled with the substances they needed to function.

Tanner and Sara decided to order room service. When it came, they talked about their days as they ate.

"So far, all I can tell you about Delilah is that she loves her little brother. It also appears that she might be doing the cooking in the family."

"I had Tim Jackson look into her background. There wasn't much to find since she's still in her teens, but he did uncover the fact that Delilah's mother is an alcoholic. The woman has been in and out of the hospital lately."

"It doesn't sound like she's involved with Niko other than as a lover. The girl is still young, she probably became a hooker so she could have enough money to take care of her brother. Niko Hyena might be a dictator who abused his own people, but he has helped Delilah. Once he's dead, she'll probably wind up prostituting herself again to survive."

"It could happen, yeah."

"It's a shame," Sara said.

Tanner looked at her. "Keep your guard up, Sara. There's still a possibility the girl could be devious. Just because she loves her brother, it doesn't mean she's not up to something or could be dangerous."

"You're right, but that's not the impression I get."

"Me neither, but I've been wrong about people before. Stay alert while you're watching her. If she has a partner, they may spot you."

"I'll be careful."

After eating, they called home to talk to the children, then settled in front of the TV to watch a movie. When it went off, they decided to go to bed early. Sara wanted to be outside the apartment house when Delilah left for the day and Tanner was meeting Henry to go over their plans to break into the estate.

∽

SARA WAS FOLLOWING DELILAH THE NEXT MORNING BY USING THE app on her phone. She was a mile behind her and assumed that she was headed toward the exit that led to the bunker. When Delilah took an earlier exit Sara wondered where she was going. Her curiosity deepened when she caught up to Delilah and noticed that her scooter was lying on its side along the curb halfway down the exit ramp. There was no sign of Delilah.

For a moment, Sara wondered if the girl had been abducted, but then she spotted her up ahead. Delilah was inside an old car with a faded vinyl top. The vehicle was sitting askew with half of its wheels up on the grass bordering the road. From Sara's viewpoint, Delilah appeared to be kissing the man behind the wheel. The seat was lowered back as far as it would go, and Delilah was straddling him.

No. Not Kissing. She was giving mouth-to-mouth resuscitation between chest compressions. Sara pulled up behind the car then got out to help.

Tears were streaming down Delilah's face, and she spoke to Sara in Spanish. "The old man needs help. Call for an ambulance."

"Let me have your phone. It will be quicker since my phone is from America and would connect with a different region than yours."

What Sara said was correct. It was also true that she still had the tracking app open on her cell phone and didn't want to risk Delilah seeing it.

Delilah dug her phone out from a side pocket of her jeans and handed it to Sara, who dialed 9-1-1. The call went through, and Sara explained what was happening.

Delilah gave a little laugh. "He's breathing again." She touched the old man's neck. "And his pulse is good but tell them to hurry."

An ambulance appeared eight minutes later and the man and woman who jumped from it went to work loading the old man into the back of their vehicle. He was a crusty old codger who smelled of cigarettes and beer, but Delilah hadn't hesitated to breathe life back into him and had shed tears over the possibility that the man, a stranger, might die. Sara decided that her instincts had been correct. Delilah was not a bad person; she had just become involved with an evil man.

As the ambulance left, she explained to Sara what had happened.

"The old man's car began swerving and I thought he might be drunk. As I came closer, I saw him clutching at his chest, then his car jumped the divider and headed down this exit, so I followed. By the time I got to the car he was passing out."

"You saved his life. What's your name?"

"Delilah Ortiz, and you?"

"I'm Sara Myers."

"You are American?"

"Yes."

When Delilah walked over to her scooter, she saw that it had a flat front tire. She had been in such a hurry to get off it and aid the old man that she hadn't noticed that she'd run over a sharp piece of metal that was lying on the side of the road.

"We'll place your scooter in the rear of my Jeep and I'll take you somewhere to get it fixed."

"Really? Thank you. That's kind of you."

"You saved a life, Delilah; I'm happy to help you," Sara said. And while handling the scooter, she would make sure to remove the tracking device. If she left it on, a mechanic might discover it.

After struggling with the scooter to place it into the Jeep, the two women got inside the vehicle.

"Where did you learn CPR?"

"In nursing school. I only went for four months but I did learn how to do that."

"Why did you leave school? You didn't like it?"

"I loved it, and I still want to be a nurse someday, but I... I had to get a job to help my mother."

"I see," Sara said.

Sara continued off the exit ramp and found that it led to a wide boulevard. Delilah told her that there was an automotive repair shop a few blocks away.

"It's on the right, next to a coffee shop. I hope they can patch my tire."

There were three young men working at the shop. They all wore smiles when they saw Delilah. Sara received looks of appreciation as well, but not as many as Delilah. Sara didn't care or notice. She was in her thirties and the mother of two children. Being thought of as less sexually desirable than a nineteen-year-old as beautiful as Delilah was only natural. And after all, the men in the shop were strangers. Who cared what they thought about anything?

The man who was running the shop said the tire couldn't be saved. He could have a new one put on the scooter within an hour or so, once one was delivered from a supplier. Delilah agreed and Sara suggested they wait in the coffee shop.

"You don't have to wait with me, Sara."

"I don't mind. I want to make sure you're all right before I leave you. And since you're a native of the city, I can ask you about places I should visit while I'm here on vacation."

Delilah agreed to have coffee, but before doing so, she wanted to make a call.

"I have to tell my boyfriend that I'll be late, or else he'll worry about me."

"I'll call my husband while you're doing that, or he may worry."

Delilah made her call to Niko while standing outside the coffee shop. Sara went inside and got a booth, then called Tanner's satellite phone. When he answered, she explained what had happened.

"You're still with her?"

"Yes. And I know it's not an ideal way to follow someone, but I couldn't leave her stranded on the highway. Cody, this girl isn't up to anything; she's just gotten involved with the wrong man and is doing her best to take care of her little brother."

"Okay. Follow her around for one more day. If you don't see anything that changes your mind about her, we'll end the surveillance."

Delilah entered the coffee shop as Sara was putting her phone away. Over the next hour they talked about the city. When Delilah learned that Sara had children, she asked to see their pictures. After looking at them, she showed Sara photos of her brother. Although she was only a decade older than Tomás, it was obvious that Delilah was doing more to raise him than their mother, and that she adored the boy.

∼

THE TIRE ON DELILAH'S SCOOTER HAD BEEN REPLACED BY THE time they returned to the garage. As Delilah paid the bill, Sara reattached the tracking device to the scooter. Afterwards, the women wished each other well and went their separate ways. Or so it appeared. After letting Delilah get back on the highway, Sara followed from a distance.

Now that she knew Delilah personally, it bothered her that the girl was involved with Niko Hyena. That the relationship wouldn't last was a given, because once Tanner killed Niko's brother, it was part of the plan that Niko would die minutes later.

Delilah would be saddened by Niko's death, but she'd be spared the life she would have lived with the one-time dictator. Sara didn't know what would come next for Delilah but feared the girl would fall back into a life of prostitution again.

She sighed. She started the day thinking that following Delilah would be boring. Instead of boredom, she felt a sense of despair. Delilah was a good person, but her future wasn't looking good, and it saddened Sara. She trailed behind Delilah as they headed toward the bunker.

20

OVER THE WALL

TANNER AND HENRY ARRIVED AT THE ESTATE AFTER MIDNIGHT then spent an hour watching for signs that it was still being guarded. There was half a moon showing in the sky along with thousands of stars.

They wore bulletproof vests and had knit caps on their heads that could be pulled down to form a mask. On Tanner's hip was a pouch that contained the explosives they would use, along with other items. Henry was toting along a black duffel bag with more supplies, such as the drill they would need. For weapons, they had handguns and short-barreled rifles hung from slings across their backs.

One man was at the compound, but he'd left and headed toward the city, likely eager to return to the celebration and feast that was going on.

"Why do you think he was here?" Henry asked.

"He could have been feeding the dogs and checking on things."

"Do you think anyone else is around?"

"We'll find out," Tanner said. "But first, let's make sure the security system has been handled." Tanner placed a call to Tim Jackson on a satellite phone.

Tim answered and said, "Are you all set to go over the wall?"

"We will be soon. First, we have to deal with the guard dogs, then you can turn the alarms off."

"Not off, they'll still activate, but I'll keep the monitoring station at the security company from knowing about it. That's the best I can do from here, Tanner, sorry."

"Don't be sorry, Tim. We couldn't do this without your help."

"We?"

"I have an apprentice with me. His name is Henry. I'll have to introduce you two sometime."

"You have a trainee? To be a hit man?"

"I prefer the term, trained assassin. And yes, someday Henry will take my place as Tanner."

"Wow. I didn't know there were such things as junior assassins. Maybe I should find someone to train as my apprentice."

"Maybe you should. You have great skill as a hacker, Tim; it should be passed along if possible."

"I'll think about that. But right now, I'll help you out. And remember, the alarms will go off and lights may flash, but no one at the alarm company will know about it."

"Wait until I call again, then do your thing. Henry and I will need time to get closer to the estate."

"You got it," Tim said.

Henry was frowning. "Did he call me a junior assassin?"

"It wasn't an insult."

"Maybe not, but I prefer the term, assassin-in-training."

They made it to the area in front of the gate but stayed far enough back so that the motion sensors built into the wall wouldn't detect them. They were also beyond the reach of the floodlights and were bathed in darkness.

Henry got down on one knee and reached into the duffel bag. When his hand came out, he was holding a slingshot and a bag of meat, along with an alarm clock.

The meat was tainted with a sedative to put the guard dogs

to sleep. The alarm clock was there to get their attention and make them all gather in one spot.

Henry held up the slingshot. "I spent the afternoon training with this sling, and it can really propel things. It would probably be deadly if you used it with something like a steel ball bearing."

"I trained on one when I was about your age, but seldom used it for anything. The same is true for the bow and arrow."

Henry loaded a small, square, travel alarm clock into the leather pouch of the sling. The clock was set inside a tough plastic case and was set to go off in two minutes. After pulling back on the sling, Henry let the clock fly. It cleared the top of the wall by only inches.

"Whoa. That was closer than I thought it would be. I'll aim higher with the chunks of meat."

Henry had delivered four of the tainted hunks of beef by the time the alarm went off and emitted a shrill buzzing sound. They never heard the dogs bark, but Henry said he heard sounds coming from beyond the wall; It was growling. When Tanner listened carefully, he detected the snarling, although it was difficult to hear over the sound the alarm clock was making.

More meat was sent over the wall and then they waited for the sedative to take effect. As they waited, they laid flat with their rifles at the ready. If there was anyone other than the dogs inside the estate, the alarm clock would have grabbed their attention as well.

Ten minutes passed with no signs of movement. During that time, the sedative should have begun working on the dogs. Beyond the wall, the growling had ceased. Tanner called Tim and told him to kill the security system's connection to the alarm company. Tim did so while still on the line and said that it was safe to proceed.

"Good luck, Tanner. And hey, let me know when you get clear again, otherwise I'll worry about you."

"I'll call, Tim, and thanks."

Tanner put the phone away and nodded at Henry. "Let's go."

They pulled down their masks to cover their faces and stepped out of the darkness. When they were within fifty feet of the wall the motion sensors detected them and alarm bells began ringing. They were so loud they drowned out the harsh buzzing sound made by the alarm clock. Additional lights blazed to life and turned the area inside the compound as bright as day. Tanner and Henry were committed to their plan to break into Kirk Hyena's safe, and a fortune in rare stamps would be their reward. The stamps were a means to an end, the end of Kirk Hyena.

~

AT THE BUNKER, KIRK WAS RECONSIDERING HIS PLAN TO HAVE Delilah killed. He had spent more time around her and saw how much his brother cared for her. The relationship had to end, but he knew if Delilah died that her death would scar Niko emotionally. Kirk loved his brother and wouldn't want to cause him undue pain. That's why he had come up with a new plan, one that would leave Delilah alive but would also reveal to Niko what a piece of lowlife trash she was. The girl was a whore. To Kirk, that made her less than human and unfit to share his brother's life.

He'd instructed Aroke to find some young stud to seduce the girl. Once Delilah took the bait, there would be photos taken of her sleeping with another man. In love or not, Kirk knew his brother would never forgive Delilah for cheating on him.

Aroke had left the bunker to fulfill that request. With the celebration going on in Juarez, there would be plenty of young men about. Paying one of them to seduce a beauty like Delilah would be like paying a bird to fly, but they would cost Kirk less money than an assassin would charge.

If Delilah was the useless slut he knew she was, she would sleep with the first good-looking man who approached her. After Niko found out, he might want to kill Delilah himself.

Kirk smiled. Now, wouldn't that be something.

∼

TANNER WAS AT THE BASE OF THE WALL AND STANDING AT THE edge of the iron gates. Beside him, Henry was removing a bundle of what looked like nylon rope from the duffel bag. They had bought a pair of fire escape ladders, the kind that clamped onto a windowsill so you could lower yourself out if a blaze occurred in a home.

The two rope ladders had been combined and had larger clamps added on along with heavy weights, which had been placed at each end of the contraption. Once he had the ladder out of the bag and untangled, Henry began spinning one end of the rope ladder around in a circle to let the weights attached to it gain momentum. It was slow going at first, but he managed to make the heavy weights spin at a good clip. When he believed the time was right, he let the weights fly. Having learned from his experience with the slingshot, he knew to aim for as high a spot as he could. It worked, but one of the weights only cleared the wall by several inches, while the second one struck the top of it before falling onto the other side.

As the weights plummeted toward the ground, they pulled the rope ladder along behind them. Sharpened clamps attached to the midpoint of the rope scraped against the wall as they slid up it, while the additional weights that were attached to the other end of the rope ladder acted as a deterrent against the whole length of the rope being yanked over. Those weights jerked, slid, but stopped moving once they slammed against the wall.

Tanner nodded with satisfaction when he saw that they had designed the contraption correctly so that there was little slack left on their side of the barrier. However, they still needed to know if the rope ladder would work as intended.

Tanner leapt up and grabbed one of the rope's rungs. His

weight caused the clamps positioned along the ladder at the top of the wall to bite into the stone beneath them. After moving a few inches, the sharp "teeth" at the ends of the clamps had bitten deep into the stone; deep enough to keep the rest of the rope ladder from being pulled back over the wall.

Henry was grinning beneath his mask. "It worked."

"Yeah. I've used something like it before. Now, let's go see if the dogs are asleep, and bring along that duffel bag."

Tanner continued up the ladder with Henry following. When he was near the top of the wall, Tanner reached out a hand toward Henry.

"Give me the duffel bag."

When he had the bag, Tanner held it by one end and slowly raised the other end over the top of the wall. Nothing happened. If someone had been waiting for a head to poke over the wall, they might have taken a shot at the bag, thinking it was a someone and not a something. He tried it again and there was still no reaction.

Tanner raised his head over the wall for an instant before ducking back down. He had seen no one nearby, and no one had taken a shot at him. After holding the bag up again and having nothing happen, Tanner tossed it over the wall, then followed it.

The dogs were asleep, with one snoring loudly. They would be out for hours and would remain groggy until the sedative left their systems completely.

Tanner jumped the last five feet to the ground and scanned the courtyard for movement while holding his rifle at the ready. Henry landed on his feet behind him and began doing the same thing. On this side of the wall the alarm sounded louder, and sight was all you had to go by. If an attacker was running up behind you, you'd be unable to detect their footfalls.

"It looks like we're alone," Tanner said into Henry's ear. "Let's move."

The ornate entrance doors of the estate were massive and had six separate locks. Tanner kept watch while Henry went to work on them. Tanner had considered using C-4 to blast their way in, but by picking the locks, it added to the impression that they were thieves, and not assassins. Besides, Henry, who had been trained to pick locks, could use the experience of working on them while under pressure.

Tanner left him to his work and concentrated on searching for movement, for a sign of a missed guard. He saw nothing. He glanced back once after enough time had passed where he knew he would have defeated all six locks. Henry had just finished with the fifth one and was moving on to the last.

Not bad, Tanner thought. He had been expecting Henry to be only up to the third lock. And while he would have been faster at the task, he also had far more experience than his apprentice.

"Done!" Henry shouted.

Tanner spun around, sent Henry a nod, and watched as the door swung open to reveal a wide entryway with a round skylight above. The half-moon was overhead and lit the space well.

Tanner brightened it further when he located and turned on the lights. There was a carved wooden bench in the foyer with a matching table and a colorful round rug. Other than that, the space was empty.

Thirty feet away was a staircase, and two flights above was the master bedroom and the safe. They headed up the stairs while moving sideways. If attacked from in front or behind, they would be ready to respond.

They reached the third floor without encountering anyone and knew that it must mean the estate was as deserted as they'd hoped it would be. That situation was about to change. Aroke was nearby. He had left the city and was headed their way.

21

YOU'RE ON YOUR OWN

Aroke had done as Kirk requested and found a young man who'd agreed to seduce Delilah. The guy was almost as pretty as Delilah but had a muscular body and drove an expensive sports car. If she were the slut Kirk believed her to be, she'd take the bait. The young stud would be paid the equivalent of a thousand American dollars when he was successful. An extra five hundred dollars ensured that the man's friend would get pictures of them together in bed.

The celebration in the city had brought in multitudes and the streets were crowded with revelers even after midnight. Aroke had one drink in a bar while he'd been hiring the gigolo, and afterwards he headed back to the car he'd taken from the bunker.

Before he returned to the bunker, he was headed to the estate to check on things. He also wanted to retrieve a book he'd started and had neglected to pack. It was boring as hell inside the bunker, and he rarely watched TV and never played video games or listened to music. He was a reader and, oddly enough, his preferred genre was westerns.

Aroke loved reading about America's old west. The fact that he was so close to Texas, where many of his favorite books had been set, made him smile. If the opportunity presented itself, he would love to visit the state. That wasn't likely to happen. As soon as it was safe to leave, Kirk would have them all headed on a jet back to Almalia.

Aroke didn't miss being back home. He had no living family there. His father having died when he was eighteen, and his mother passed away when he was three. There was also no woman to return to. He was considered an outcast among his people because his father had served the dictator, Tristan Nilsson. And now, Aroke served his replacements, Kirk and Niko Hyena.

Although he knew he would never be seen as an equal by either man, Aroke thought of them as his brothers. They had grown up together and shared many experiences, and even girls. Once they reached adulthood, their different social status became more pronounced and Aroke had found himself being excluded from the boys' lives.

They were treated like princes and he like the son of a guard that he was. He'd always gotten along better with Kirk than Niko. Niko had been like his little brother while they were growing up but had begun treating him like a servant by the time they'd reached puberty. When he saved the brothers from being killed, they had been grateful, and Kirk had started treating him more like an equal.

Aroke didn't consider himself to be their equal. He'd had the servant mentality drummed into him since the day he was born and bought into the lie that Tristan Nilsson and his sons were his betters. He was a guard, a defender, and if it cost him his life, he would defend Kirk and Niko against any threat.

∽

HE REALIZED THERE WAS A PROBLEM AT THE ESTATE BEFORE HE reached it. There were too many lights ablaze. When he drew closer and detected the sound of the alarm blaring, he pulled the car over and took out his phone.

There was no signal. Of course, there was no signal this far away from the city. Aroke cursed himself for neglecting to bring along a satellite phone. He considered turning around and driving until he acquired a signal, but then thought better of it. Even if he reached one of the cartel thugs who normally guarded the estate, it was likely they were drunk or asleep. By the time they got themselves together and made it out to the estate, whoever had broken in would be long gone.

Or maybe they had already left, which was as likely as anything else. If it was an assassin out to kill Kirk, they had chosen the wrong time to make their move. Kirk was safe and out of reach inside the bunker.

His decision made, Aroke continued driving toward the estate. When he was parking outside the gate, he spotted the rope ladder. He left his vehicle while holding a gun and walked over to the ladder. Aroke held his phone in his left hand and used it as a flashlight to study the ground near the bottom of the ladder; he could see that there were two sets of boot prints in the sand. There were fresh prints leading to the rope but none leading away. The intruders were still inside.

Aroke yanked on the ladder. He'd been hoping to pull it back over and leave the intruders trapped behind the wall. It was a wasted effort. The clamps at the top of the wall were holding the ladder firmly in place.

After putting away his phone he began climbing awkwardly. His movements were jerky because he was keeping a grip on his gun and only using his left hand to pull himself up the ladder. When he was at the top, he saw the drugged dogs and the open doors at the front of the home.

Knowing he'd have to turn his back on the doors to climb down, Aroke reluctantly holstered his weapon and hurried down the rope as fast as he could. When he reached bottom, he lowered himself into a crouch and scanned his surroundings with his weapon back in his hand. Seeing no movement, he headed toward the open doors.

Upon entering the house, Aroke studied the alarm panel to the left of the door and saw that the alarm had first sounded eight minutes earlier. The alarm was deafening, and he was reaching up to input the code that would silence it when he stopped himself. If he silenced the alarm, he would be announcing his presence. Outnumbered two to one, surprise was his main advantage, and he would use it to kill or capture whoever had broken into the estate.

As Aroke eased up the steps, he heard a muffled explosion come from somewhere above.

~

TANNER AND HENRY ROSE FROM THEIR PLACE OF COVER BEHIND A sofa and walked over to look at the safe. The explosive had done its job and the lock on the safe was destroyed. Tanner yanked on the safe's handle and swung the door open while standing to the side. If Kirk Hyena had rigged some sort of booby trap it could be arranged in such a way to injure anyone who opened the door while standing in front of it.

There was no trap but there was a light that came on after the safe door had opened several inches. The light had been activated by the motion of the moving door and illuminated the contents of the safe. Tanner peeked around the edge of the door and saw stacks of money, a tray lined with black velvet that had several gold watches laying upon it, and a file folder full of papers. He ignored it all and kept searching with his eyes. When he spotted a leather-bound album lying on a narrow shelf at the top of the safe, he made a grunt of satisfaction. Using a flashlight, Tanner checked to see if there was a wire or anything else attached to the album, or perhaps a sensor plate beneath it. There was nothing but the album, although lying beside it were stamp hinges, glassine strips, clear plastic sleeves, and other items that were used to mount stamps inside an album.

Tanner took the album from the safe, and as he removed it, he felt a device inside his pocket vibrate. He turned to Henry and mouthed the words.

"We've got company."

∼

THE VIBRATION TANNER FELT CAME FROM A RECEIVER THAT WAS linked to three separate motion detectors he had placed at the base of the railing along the stairs. Aroke had set one off on his way up without realizing it.

He had recognized that the explosion he'd heard had been someone blowing open Kirk's safe. That marked the intruders as being thieves. Before that, he had wondered if he was dealing with assassins. Crooks or killers, their fate would be the same, he would fire on them at first sight and question anyone who survived their wounds.

The constant sound of the alarm was irritating but also reassured him that his approach couldn't be heard as he neared the master bedroom. The door was sitting ajar, and he could see flashes of light coming from within. Aroke reached out a hand to push the door inward when he was struck on the back of his head. He let out a groan as he fell to his knees but held on to his gun. A second blow made him see stars before everything faded to black.

∼

TANNER FLIPPED AROKE ONTO HIS BACK TO LOOK AT HIS FACE. HE recognized him from a photo that had been supplied by Thomas Lawson and knew that Aroke was Kirk Hyena's right-hand man. He speculated over the reason why Aroke had been at the estate so late at night and wondered if he had come alone.

After claiming Aroke's weapon, Tanner used the man's flashlight to signal to Henry that it was safe to leave the room. Henry appeared holding the duffel bag. Inside it was Kirk's stamp collection, twenty-five thousand dollars and an equivalent value in pesos. They had also taken the watches. They were gold and antique timepieces that had once belonged to Tristan Nilsson.

While pointing down at Aroke, Tanner spoke into Henry's ear to be understood over the alarm. He made a mental note to have Henry learn sign language. It would have made communicating easier in this situation and might come in handy in the future.

"He might not be alone; stay alert as we leave."

Henry nodded his understanding and they moved along the corridor and toward the stairs. Since Aroke had been alone, they encountered no one else. Ten minutes later, they were back in their vehicles and headed for their hotel. Stage one of Tanner's plan had been accomplished. Now, it was up to Kirk Hyena to take the bait.

~

KIRK LEARNED ABOUT THE ROBBERY AFTER AROKE CALLED AND woke him up in the early morning hours. He was livid at what he took to be a personal offense and swore he'd see the thieves dead. To that end, he contacted the man he dealt with inside the cartel. When he explained the situation, Kirk was stunned by the man's reply.

"You're on your own. It was your property that was stolen, and the cartel won't go after the thieves."

"I'm paying you a fortune for protection. What do you mean you won't hunt down the thieves?"

The man chuckled. "You don't understand, do you? You're lucky to still have access to the hacienda and the bunker. After what your brother did to Hernando, there were some that wanted him dead, and you with him. If you had refused to pay the fee they charged, they would have killed you."

"Hernando is a lowlife pimp."

"Yeah, but he's also the nephew of a man high up in the cartel. You'll still be protected but don't expect any help getting your baseball cards back."

Kirk gripped the phone tighter. "They're not baseball cards; they are rare stamps and worth over two million dollars."

"Next time get a better safe," the man said, then hung up.

22
A RANSOM DEMAND

Aroke had a lump on the back of his head the size of a golf ball, a headache that wouldn't go away, and was dizzy. These were signs he had suffered a concussion; however, he was able to move about slowly, as the vertigo wasn't severe.

After regaining his senses, Aroke had reset the alarm after removing the rope ladder from the wall and checking on the dogs.

He'd driven into the city where he located several of the guards and informed them that their time off was being cut short. He left the area only after he was certain that there were enough guards in place. He'd also had the security company send someone to do a sweep for listening devices and hidden cameras, or explosives. Just because he assumed it was thieves who'd stolen the stamps didn't mean he wouldn't take precautions. The robbery could have been a cover for something else. When the sweep came up clean, he was again certain they were dealing with only thieves. Whoever they were, they weren't common crooks. They had targeted the safe and left everything else untouched, although there had been laptops, cameras, and other valuable items lying around.

Aroke made it back to the bunker in the afternoon and met

with Kirk inside the bedroom Kirk was using. He told Kirk he was certain there were two thieves and that they must have a knowledge of security systems since they had managed to keep their alarm from communicating with the security company's monitoring station.

"They were professionals, Kirk. That means they've done this before. The cartel will be able to find them when the thieves attempt to fence your stamps."

Kirk made a face of disgust. "The cartel won't help. It's punishment for what Niko did to that pimp."

Aroke sucked in air through his teeth. "Without their help and their connections with the law, it will be difficult to find these men."

"What did you do with the papers I keep in the safe?"

"I brought them here as you asked. They're inside a laptop bag that's sitting on the coffee table in the living room."

Kirk looked relieved. "If the thieves had stolen those and given them to the wrong people, I would never be allowed to return to Almalia. Those hypocrites at the U.N. would label me and Niko as war criminals."

Aroke didn't know what Kirk was talking about and didn't want to know. It was his job to protect the man, not judge him or his actions.

Kirk's satellite phone rang. When he answered it, he heard the voice of one of the cartel thugs who guarded him at the estate. The man had news.

~

"A COURIER? WHAT IS HE DELIVERING?"

After listening for a response, Kirk spoke to Aroke. "Head back to the estate. There's been an envelope delivered. The person who sent it claims to be 'A fellow stamp collector.'"

"You think it has something to do with the robbery?"

"It must, but I don't know what games the thieves could be playing."

"Maybe they've realized you're connected to the cartel and became afraid to fence the stamps. They could be offering to sell them back to you."

"Go get that envelope and bring it here, Aroke. Maybe I'll get my stamps back after all."

∼

AROKE RETURNED WITH THE ENVELOPE. ON HIS WAY BACK, HE'D stopped at the courier service to gather a description of the man who sent the envelope. The clerk told him that it had been dropped off by a woman. That woman had been Sara, who had worn sunglasses, along with a hat with a wide brim that hid her face from the cameras. The clerk did tell Aroke that he believed the woman was an American, judging by her accent.

Kirk opened the envelope and found a typed letter written in English. Along with the letter was a stamp—one of his stamps. It wasn't his most valuable, but it was worth more than most cars, and he was relieved to have regained possession of it. He read the note.

To the owner of the stamps. If you want them back, we can make it happen for twenty-five million pesos. The stamp in the envelope is a gesture of good faith. We will be in touch soon.

Kirk was grinning by the time he finished the note. They hadn't referred to him by name and were willing to make an exchange of cash for the stamps. Twenty-five million pesos was around a million dollars in American money. He wouldn't pay a dime of it, but he would make sure that he got his stamps back and killed the thieves.

Aroke asked what the note said. He could speak English, as he had learned the language from Kirk and Niko while they were growing up, but he'd never been formally taught English as they had and couldn't read it well. Aroke's native language was a mixture of Arabic and Swahili, and like many people in Africa, he spoke French.

When Kirk explained what was written in the note, Aroke understood why he was smiling.

"When they show up to make the exchange, we'll have men waiting for them."

"Yes, we will. But they'll be ready for that. We'll use men, but I'll also want you nearby with a rifle. How far away can you be and still remain accurate?"

"If I have the right weapon, one kilometer. There's a weapon back at the estate that will do the job."

Kirk clapped him on the shoulder. "Get that weapon. And you'll use it to kill the men who dared to rob me."

"They may choose a location that offers no concealment. If so, I'll have to wear camouflage of some sort."

"Do whatever it takes, but I want you to have everything ready by tonight; they may make contact again before tomorrow." Kirk took out his wallet and removed a credit card. "Use that to buy what you need and stay in touch."

Aroke had his hand on the doorknob when Kirk called to him. "What about that other matter?"

"The girl? It's all set. The man I picked will approach her later today."

"Is the guy good-looking?"

Aroke walked back over with his phone and showed Kirk a photo of a handsome young man with long hair and lots of muscle.

Kirk laughed. "He's like a male version of Delilah; she'll bed him for sure."

"What if she doesn't?"

"Then, she'll just have to have a tragic accident. Maybe something involving that stupid scooter of hers."

"I've been asking around. There's a man who arranges accidents. His fee is ten thousand dollars."

"A Mexican?"

"Yeah."

"Hire him if it becomes necessary, and then afterwards, kill him too. I can't have this traced back to me."

"Maybe it won't be necessary; the girl was a prostitute. She'll probably sleep with anyone who asks."

"I hope so. I don't want to kill her if I don't have to. It would break Niko's heart. Still, I can't have him tie himself to a woman like that. She's beneath him."

Aroke headed for the door again. "I'll have my satellite phone with me. Call me if you need me."

"I will. And bring back some food, real food. I can't stand those frozen dinners that Niko eats."

Aroke smiled and left to run his errands, like the lackey he was.

23
ASHES

TANNER ARRANGED TO MEET WITH KIRK AT A SECLUDED SPOT IN the desert that was south of the estate. There were hills in the area, and from those hills you could spot the roofs of buildings that were in a small town if you used a pair of binoculars.

It was also true that you could see what was going on atop the hills if you were on one of those roofs with a camera that had zoom capability. Tanner and Henry were on one such roof and doing just that.

It was Tanner who spotted Aroke first. Aroke was situated on the tallest hill and was in a prone position. Instead of being out in the open, he was hidden beneath a blanket that was the same color of the ground he was lying on. Tanner had spotted the tip of the rifle Aroke was using and assumed there was a scope attached to it. The rifle was aimed at the spot in the desert where the exchange was to take place.

Kirk was to show up at noon with twenty-five million pesos in cash and exchange the money for his stamp collection, and only his stamp collection. Tanner had made it clear to Kirk in a second message he'd sent that he was keeping the valuable watches and the money found in the safe. The money could be used anywhere, and the watches were easily exchanged for cash on online auction sites or even a pawn shop. As for the stamps, while they could be cashed in, it would take time. Money was accepted everywhere, and many people wanted antique watches, not everyone wanted a rare stamp. Converting them to cash could take months and, because of their rarity, the buyer might realize they'd been stolen and alert the authorities. It would be much easier all around to sell them back to their rightful owner.

This was how the real Ransom Bandits operated according to Caleb. Since Tanner and Henry were pretending to be the infamous pair of thieves, they copied their modus operandi. Kirk sent one of his guards to the site of the meeting in his place. The man was dressed in a suit and tie and was holding the handle of a suitcase that had wheels. The suitcase was big enough to contain the twenty-five million in pesos but was empty. Kirk had no intention of paying to get his own stamps back, not when it was easier to kill the thieves and take the stamps from their dead hands.

Tanner was aware of that and was letting Kirk renege on the deal so he could take his plan to the next stage. Kirk wasn't ready to pay yet and would do everything possible to avoid parting with the money. However, he'd be more than ready to pay whatever was asked by the end, and when that end point came, he'd be desperate to get his property back.

Henry made an observation. "The guy with the rifle might be the same guy who was at the estate the other night. The file on him said that he was an excellent marksman."

"It's probably him. His name is Aroke Okoro. Kirk Hyena would trust him to bring his stamps back."

"How long are you going to make them wait?"

"Forever, but they'll probably wait another hour before giving up and leaving. Later, they'll know about the package Sara is sending for me."

Henry grinned. "Kirk Hyena is going to be pissed when he sees what you've done."

"Yeah, but he'll realize we're serious and that he can't easily kill us and get his stamps back."

"You think he'll show up at the next meeting?"

"I doubt it. My guess is he'll make at least one more attempt to outsmart us. He's used to being in control. It will take a lot to get him to the point of panic that I want him in. I'll let him play games a little longer, then I'll hit him with something that will make him realize he has to risk himself if he wants to get his property back."

Henry gazed through the lens of the camera again. The guy in the suit pretending to be Kirk Hyena was looking at his watch. The time for the meeting had come and gone.

Tanner took out a phone and sent off a text to Sara.

It's time to send the package.

∽

IN JUAREZ, SARA RECEIVED THE TEXT AND WAS READY TO DO HER part. She was following Delilah again. The girl had just dropped her little brother off at school and would be headed toward the bunker to spend time with Niko.

Sara didn't need to watch Delilah but had decided to do so anyway. Why, she didn't know, but had felt the impulse and followed it. She had learned nothing new and was still of the opinion that Delilah was a good person who was headed down a bad path. After she sent off the package for Tanner, Sara would head to the bunker, where she would keep watch for several hours. If Kirk or Niko left the bunker, she would let Tanner know about it.

As Delilah walked back to her scooter to climb on, a red sports car pulled up beside her. The man driving the car had the good looks of a male model. When he left the vehicle to approach Delilah, Sara saw that he was tall, muscular, and dressed in designer jeans. There was a gold necklace gleaming around his neck and given the sparkle coming off his watch, it was also made of gold.

Sara was too far away to hear what was being said but experience told her that the man was hitting on Delilah. The girl was shaking her head as she straddled her bike, but the man persisted with his attempt at seduction. Given how good-looking he was, Sara doubted he'd been turned down often, if ever.

After Delilah put on her helmet, she started up her scooter. The man stood in front of it, attempting to block her way, when a teacher at the school walked over. She was a motherly type who must have known Delilah through her brother, or perhaps Delilah had attended the same school herself years earlier.

The teacher shooed the man away and stood there until he drove off. Before leaving, Delilah gave the woman a hug.

Sara smiled. It appeared that Delilah was faithful to Niko. It was one more reason for her to like the girl. Before heading to the bunker to keep watch, Sara had a package to send off. She would use a different courier service than the one she had used the last time, but still took the precaution of wearing the wide-brimmed hat and sunglasses. Instead of just a note, Kirk Hyena would receive something of substance to let him know that the men who'd stolen his stamps weren't playing games.

∼

THE PACKAGE ARRIVED AT THE ESTATE AND AROKE WAS SENT TO fetch it. He had made the trip between the bunker and the estate so many times over the last few days that it was beginning to feel like a commute.

Kirk was already angry because nothing had happened at the meeting site. When he received word that a package had been delivered, he felt like the thieves were taunting him. When he opened the package, he found a cell phone and a sealed white envelope. There was also a note.

Nice try using the man with the rifle to kill us, but we aren't stupid enough to walk into a trap. If you want these stamps back, pay up. Otherwise, you'll never see them again. We'll call you on the enclosed phone later today to set up another meeting.

PS—There was a penalty to pay. Open the envelope.

Kirk looked at the phone. It was a cheap burner that could have been purchased anywhere. It wouldn't work inside the bunker. He'd have to send Aroke outside and closer to the city for the thing to work.

When he opened the envelope, he saw that it contained three smaller envelopes; they were numbered 1, 2, and 3. The first envelope contained a photo of a stamp that was a part of his collection and was valued at around twenty-five thousand dollars. The word BEFORE was written at the top of the picture. Kirk tore open the second envelope and found another photo. It had the word AFTER written over a picture of a small scattering of ash. That ash was found when Kirk opened the final envelope. When he realized his stamp had been burned, Kirk turned crimson with anger, yelled an obscenity, and kicked over a chair. The note had said that a penalty had been paid. The stamp was that penalty. And it was a stamp that had once belonged to Kirk's father.

Niko had been in his bedroom playing video games while waiting for Delilah to arrive. He came running and asked his brother what was wrong.

"The thieves destroyed one of my stamps." Kirk raised his hands and made claws of them. "If they were standing here right now, I would strangle them."

"I thought that was being handled today. What happened?"

"They never showed. They spotted Aroke and realized it was a trap."

Niko frowned at Aroke. "You should have remained hidden until they appeared."

"There was nowhere to hide, but I was camouflaged and a kilometer away from the meeting site. These men, the thieves, they are not amateurs. I suggest that next time we use more men."

Kirk startled when Aroke used the words, "next time." The thieves would be calling, and someone had to answer the phone he'd been given. He handed it to Aroke.

"Take this and head out until you get a strong signal. When the call comes in, listen carefully to what is said. We may only get one more chance at these men."

"Should I pretend to be you?"

"Yes. And agree to anything they want. You're right; next time we'll use more men, and we'll be trickier as well."

Aroke was heading for a tunnel to leave when Delilah was arriving at the bunker's main entrance. When Niko left the room to let her inside, Kirk gave Aroke more instructions.

"Find out if the little whore cheated on my brother. If she didn't, then hire that assassin you told me about."

Aroke said he understood and headed into an escape tunnel. A few minutes later, when Kirk greeted Delilah's arrival, he smiled at her and said it was good to see her again. He'd always been an excellent liar.

24

FLUSH 'EM OUT

Tanner hadn't actually burned the rare stamp. The ashes he'd sent Kirk had been those of an average postage stamp that was worth less than a dollar.

Knowing that the cell phone he'd given to Kirk would be useless in the area where the bunker was located, Tanner assumed Kirk would send Aroke out of the bunker with the phone. He did, and Tanner and Henry followed Aroke from a distance. Although it looked like a cheap phone, the device he'd sent Kirk allowed Tanner to track whoever was holding it with the assistance of a satellite. It also had a microphone so Tanner could listen in to any discussions that went on.

Despite that, the phone hadn't worked underground inside the bunker, so he and Henry had never heard the conversation between Kirk and Aroke, where Kirk gave Aroke the go ahead to hire someone to kill Delilah. Had he known about that, Tanner would have done something to prevent it.

~

Aroke drove toward the city. When he was certain the phone had a good connection to a cell tower, he pulled into the parking lot of a shopping center. He had no idea how long he'd have to wait before a call came in, and the shopping center offered a place where he could get food or use a toilet.

While he was waiting, he called the man he had hired to seduce Delilah. He was surprised when he learned of his failure and also saddened. It would have been much better for Niko if Delilah had betrayed him. Her death would wound him deeper than if she had simply been unfaithful.

The decision to have her killed was Kirk's, but Aroke was the one who would see that it was done. He removed a laptop from a case and sent off a message to an assassin who was an expert at arranging accidents.

A reply came in. Then a payment was arranged and details about Delilah were provided, including a photo of the girl, along with her habits. Aroke was aware that Delilah left the bunker each weekday in the afternoon so she could pick up her brother from school. She also drove the boy there on the back of her scooter. Her probable routes were written down.

When the assassin saw Delilah's photo, he responded with the words, "What a waste."

When Aroke asked when the deed would be done, the assassin typed in the reply, "Within three days the young lady will have an unfortunate traffic accident."

Aroke assured the assassin that the remainder of his payment would be forwarded when Delilah was dead and closed his laptop.

The burner phone rang as he was about to leave his vehicle to get something to eat. When Aroke answered it, he heard Tanner speak in English.

"Are you George Harper?"

George Harper was the alias Kirk was using. If the thieves were referring to Kirk by that name, it meant they had no idea who he really was. And despite Aroke's limited knowledge of American accents, he could recognize that Tanner was speaking with a southern drawl.

"I am Harper. I want to meet and get my stamps back."

"Name six of the stamps in your collection."

Aroke cursed under his breath. All he knew about Kirk's stamps was that they were valuable. He couldn't name one of them.

"You can't name them, can you? You're not George Harper."

"I am Mr. Harper's bodyguard, Aroke. He wants another opportunity to get his stamps back."

Tanner chuckled. "I bet he does, but it won't happen if he keeps playing games and attempts to have us killed."

"He will have the money and an exchange will take place. I know a good spot where we can do it."

"Uh-uh, we get to pick the spot, and we'll use the same one as last time. And I want Harper there in person; I'll only hand the stamps over to him."

"Why does that matter?"

"Because if he comes to the exchange, it will put him in danger if he attempts to cheat us again."

"Cheat you? How can someone cheat a thief? You stole the stamps and demand extortion money to return them. You are the cheat!"

"I guess it's all in how you look at things, but the bottom line is that Harper will never see his stamps again if we don't get our money. I know the guy is mega rich; he'd have to be to own a fortune in rare stamps and live in an estate like the one we robbed. What we're asking should be nothing to him."

"When do you want to meet?"

"The exchange will go down at midnight tonight. Tell Harper if he tries any tricks, I'll destroy another stamp."

"I'll tell him, but he won't come alone. There are two of you."

"You can tag along with your boss and hold his hand. But just you. If we see anyone else there, we'll call off the meeting. Any questions?"

"Yes. Are you the one who struck me from behind like a coward?"

"That was me. If we'd been facing each other, you wouldn't have done any better."

"Maybe we'll find out someday."

"I doubt it. I'll be wearing a ski mask tonight and you'll never see my face. And after your boss pays up, I'll be leaving Mexico for a nice vacation on a tropical island, and I'll have plenty of money to enjoy myself."

Aroke gripped the phone tighter as he gritted his teeth. He'd always hated thieves, and he owed the man on the phone for hurting him.

"Come to the meeting tonight. There will be no tricks."

"Yeah," Tanner said. "We'll see," and then the call ended.

Aroke changed his mind about getting something to eat; his appetite had deserted him.

∼

Tanner and Henry were in the city and having lunch. Tanner had made the call from the booth they were sitting in.

Henry had listened to the call and was chuckling. "It sounds like Aroke is mad. If his boss doesn't try something tricky, he will."

"Kirk Hyena will be setting up some sort of ambush, and we've given him plenty of time to do so. It will also give us time to get ready."

"What do you want to do? Normally, I would say we should show up there with night vision and take out his guards one at a time, but if we did that, Hyena would know we were really assassins."

"That's right. So, we'll make them expose the trap they set without walking into it."

"How do we do that?"

Tanner pointed out the window to a men's clothing store that was across the street. The two mannequins in the window were dressed in suits. "We need to go shopping."

Aroke called Kirk using a satellite phone. Kirk instructed him to return to the estate and gather up the men who had recently returned from celebrating in the city. There were over a dozen of them. The rest would be back on duty the next day when Kirk would be leaving the bunker.

Three men were to head out to the meeting site and keep watch while the others prepared themselves. Two hours before the midnight deadline, the men were to gather in vehicles near the area and form a loose perimeter watch.

"Make sure they know not to smoke or talk loudly or do anything else that would give them away."

"They'll still be visible; there is nowhere out there to hide," Aroke said.

"Place them far enough away so that it won't matter, maybe as far as three kilometers. When a vehicle comes near the meeting site, then send out a group text telling the men to move in. The important thing is to lure the thieves into the trap."

"That should work. And that far out from the meeting site there are small hills and a patch of trees that should conceal the men. There are a couple of them that have motorcycles; I'll have them bring them. It will give us more maneuverability in case the thieves slip out of the trap."

"Make sure they don't. And if possible, take both alive. I'll enjoy torturing them."

"I will help you. I owe them for hurting me."

"No mistakes this time, Aroke, understood?"

"No mistakes. We'll get your stamps back."

"Do so and I'll give you a bonus. What about the girl, did she sleep with that Casanova you hired?"

"No. He approached her this morning and was turned down. I went ahead and hired the killer. He expects to murder her sometime over the next three days. It will look like she had an accident."

Kirk sighed. "Poor Niko will be saddened by her death. But I know my brother, within a month he'll be sleeping with other women again, and a year from now, Delilah will only be a memory."

"By then we'll be back in Almalia. I look forward to leaving Mexico; there's been nothing but trouble since we got here."

"We'll return home once my enemies are dead. Now, get busy and set up the trap. These thieves will learn a lesson tonight, and I'll get my stamps back."

~

WITH MIDNIGHT APPROACHING, AROKE STOOD IN THE MIDDLE OF an empty plain under the stars. Standing beside him was one of the guards pretending to be Kirk. With them was the suitcase that was supposed to be filled with cash. There was no cash, but neither was the bag empty. There were two rifles inside it equipped with silencers. When the thieves showed up for the meeting, Aroke and the man beside him would open the bag and arm themselves. All the other men, those out of sight among the surrounding terrain, carried weapons that also had sound suppressors. Being close to the road and the town, they didn't want to attract attention if shooting began.

There had been several false alarms as cars passed by on the nearby road, either on their way to or returning from Juarez. The town had a small population and being close to midnight there wasn't much traffic.

Minutes later, Aroke was beginning to wonder if something had gone wrong. His watch was telling him that it was eleven past midnight and the thieves had still not appeared. He breathed a sigh of relief when he saw headlights approaching from his left, where the highway was off in the distance. The thieves must have driven across the scrubland instead of using the road that led to the town.

It was a smart move but wouldn't save them. Once they passed a certain point, there would be no way for them to escape the trap they were entering. When that moment arrived, Aroke took out his phone and sent off a text he had already typed out.

Move in now but do not fire until I give the signal. And leave your lights off.

The headlights were getting closer, but Aroke still couldn't make out what sort of vehicle it was. He sent a text to one of the men on the motorcycles who had been positioned out in the desert.

What are they driving?

The man responded. *It is a pickup truck, A Ford Raptor. There are two men in the front wearing ski masks.*

The Raptor was an expensive vehicle, and being thieves, Aroke figured it had been stolen to use for the meeting. The truck was moving toward Aroke and the man beside him on an angle as it trundled along over the sandy terrain. It easily mowed over the scrub brush it encountered. Aroke looked beyond the truck, to his right and left, then behind him and saw dark shapes moving. They were the cartel members closing in.

As the pickup truck came closer, Aroke saw that it wasn't slowing, but then, it had only been going about twenty miles an hour. The vehicle kept advancing and he saw the two masked figures in the front seat as they passed by him. They must have spotted the other vehicles moving toward them and were seeking to escape.

The truck was on his left and a dozen yards away when Aroke opened the case at his feet and removed a rifle. After taking aim, he blew apart a rear tire. By firing his weapon, he had given the signal that the truck was fair game.

The other men were under orders to target the vehicle's tires. If a bullet entered the cab and tore through a stamp there would be hell to pay. If they were fired upon by the men inside the truck, then they could defend themselves.

More men fired at the truck; its tires were ripped apart and it continued to lumber along. After failing to make it up and over a sand dune, the truck flipped, rolled over once, and settled on its side. Aroke got to the truck on a run as one of the cartel thugs broke a window to reach inside and drag the driver out. When only a head and torso emerged, Aroke wondered if the driver had somehow been severed in half during the truck's rollover. He had still been processing that thought when another part of his mind noticed the lack of blood.

When the same man pulled a pair of legs from the truck while saying the word, "Mannequin," in Spanish, Aroke knew he had been outsmarted and had failed once again. No one had been driving the truck, the wheels of which were still turning. When Aroke looked inside, he saw that a metal bar had been secured well. It extended from the front of the seat to the gas pedal. The length of the bar was enough to exert a steady pressure that had maintained the truck's speed. The "two men" riding in the front were mannequins wearing dark clothing and ski masks.

As he hung his head in disgust, Aroke heard a phone ring. The sound was coming from the phone he'd called the thieves on earlier. He answered it with a sigh and spoke one word.

"Yes?"

Tanner's voice came over the line, once again he was speaking with a southern accent. He had no idea if Kirk Hyena would be aware of the real Ransom Bandits, but if he was, it was best to imitate the pair as much as possible, right down to their pattern of speech. "Tell your boss he's not as smart as he thinks he is, and check the center console in the truck. I'll wait."

Aroke told one of the men to look inside the console. The man crawled into the truck. When he came out, he handed Aroke an envelope. Aroke didn't need to open it to know what was inside.

"These are more ashes, aren't they?" he said into the phone.

"That's right. And we're done playing games. Your boss has

until three p.m. to get the money together. I'll call at three and tell him where to meet me. And Aroke, I'll want to speak to him, not you. He can bring you along to our meeting, and one other man, but no more, and I'll give him until tomorrow at midnight to get to me. If he shows up with more than two men or is late, he'll never see his stamps again. Do we understand each other?"

"I understand your terms and will repeat them to my boss, but he could use more time to gather the money together."

"He's already had more than a day. It's not my fault he chose to waste his time."

"He'll have the money."

There was no answer, then Aroke realized his caller had hung up. A phone rang again, but this time it was the satellite phone. It was Kirk calling to see how things had gone. Aroke closed his eyes as he answered.

"I have bad news, Kirk."

∼

TANNER AND HENRY HAD BEEN WATCHING THE ACTION FROM THE same roof they'd been on during the first aborted exchange. They had set up the stunt with the pickup truck earlier and had used chunks of ice to act as wheel chocks. When the ice had melted enough, the truck began moving. It had been a tough thing to time correctly, which was the reason the truck reached the meeting place late.

From where they were, it looked as if Aroke and the other men had shredded the car with gunfire, as dozens of flashes had been observed.

"Whoever owned that truck we stole will not be happy," Henry said.

"I'll make it up to him by giving him the watches we took from the safe. They're worth enough that he'll be able to buy three or four of those trucks."

Tanner put away his camera and headed for the ladder that

was attached to the side of the building, which contained a store that sold mattresses.

"Let's go get a good night's sleep; tomorrow is the big day. When I call Kirk at three p.m. everything will get rolling, and by four o'clock, both Hyena brothers will be dead."

25

TOO CLEVER FOR YOUR OWN GOOD

THE NEXT MORNING, KIRK HYENA WAS BACK INSIDE THE ESTATE after making the return trip surrounded by his full retinue of guards. Delilah had come by early to say goodbye to him. Kirk had to force himself to be polite and smile. A true grin appeared on his face when he remembered the girl would be dead soon.

That grin was long gone now, and he was angrier than he had ever been. He believed that another of his valuable stamps had been destroyed and he had been outmaneuvered by the thieves again.

When Aroke asked him if he was considering paying the thieves to get back the stamps, Kirk shouted at him.

"Not one damn cent! Do you hear me? I won't pay one damn cent. And next time I'll go to the meeting in person."

"Kirk, remember that there is an assassin out there somewhere who's waiting to take a shot at you. If you do what the thieves ask and go to the meeting with only two men, it will be hard to protect you properly."

"I'll be in a bulletproof limo."

"That will be fine while we're traveling, but what about once we reach our destination?"

"We'll make sure no one follows us. Whatever. All I care

about is getting those stamps back before another one is destroyed."

"I find something odd."

"What's that?"

"There are two thieves, but he's allowing you to bring two men with you. That means we'll outnumber them by 3-to-2. Why would they handicap themselves that way?"

"Maybe he wants to make me feel more confident about meeting in person."

"Maybe, or maybe there's another reason. They could be planning to kill the third man to show us that they're serious. If that happens, and they figure out we didn't bring money, they may try to kill us."

Kirk was shaking his head. "These men are thieves, not killers. If they were dangerous, they could have killed you the other night. They didn't even harm the dogs. Instead of poisoning the hounds, they only drugged them."

"True, but it's odd that they would allow you an advantage."

Kirk checked his watch. "We'll have to leave here in an hour or two and head toward the city where the phone will get a signal. Make sure the driver is a man who is good with a gun. We'll also have him check for anyone who might try to follow us. When the call comes in and we know where to go, we'll come back here and gather a group of the men together to follow us. If trouble does break out, we'll have someone backing us up."

"I'm bringing along extra weapons and ammunition tonight."

"Do that," Kirk said, as he freed a knife from a sheath that hung from his belt. "And when we have the thieves, I'm going to use this blade to torture them. They'll wish they had never stepped foot inside this house."

~

TANNER HAD GIVEN SARA A PART TO PLAY IN HIS PLAN. SHE WAS ready to do it but found herself preoccupied with Delilah. For some reason, she couldn't shake the feeling that she should continue to follow the girl. When Tanner told her of the conversation he'd overheard Aroke have with someone on the phone concerning Delilah, Sara assumed it had been with the young man who had attempted to seduce the girl.

Since Kirk wasn't the sort to give up easily, he would attempt some other way to separate Delilah from his brother, Niko. He had already tried the carrot approach, maybe next time he'd use the stick.

Sara had been near the bunker after following Delilah there, and she had seen Kirk's departure in the limousine surrounded by his hoard of cartel thugs.

As three o'clock approached, Sara needed to leave her observation post to get into position to help Tanner make his plan a success. As she was preparing to leave, Delilah exited the bunker and headed for her scooter. Sara wanted to follow her but couldn't or she risked being unable to fulfill her part of the plan.

While she couldn't trail after Delilah, she was able to keep her in sight for a while by using the scope on the rifle she had with her. It was while doing so that she saw the man in the pickup truck leave his place of concealment and speed toward Delilah. They were in an area where the trail through the desert was on a narrow ridge that had a drop-off to its left. A fall from there would be in excess of seventy feet at its highest point. Within seconds, the truck had gained on the scooter and was inches from its rear wheel. A moment more and it made contact, jolting Delilah. Delilah hadn't known the truck was there until it struck her. The truck's engine noise had been undetected because of the loudness of the scooter's own engine and the helmet Delilah was wearing.

The truck accelerated and struck the scooter again, which caused Delilah to lose control. Delilah fell from the scooter, slid across sand, and smashed into a lump of rock headfirst. Had she not been wearing the helmet, her skull would have cracked wide open. Instead, she was knocked unconscious. That outcropping of rock had saved her life; had it not been there, Delilah would have rolled off the edge of the trail and fallen to her death.

~

THE ASSASSIN OUT TO KILL DELILAH WAS NAMED GARCIA. HE'D been active for six years and had arranged dozens of accidents. He'd decided that making it look like Delilah had died from a fall after losing control of her scooter would be the simplest way to kill her. Too simple really, as he preferred setting up more complicated and dramatic deaths, such as blowing up a target's house and making it appear that their water heater had exploded. Suicides were good too, and he often made those he'd been paid to kill take a tumble from a roof. The cliff wasn't a rooftop, but the fall from its height would end the girl's life all the same when she slammed into the rocks below. Garcia sighed as he stared at Delilah's unmoving form. The girl was a beauty, and it seemed a shame to kill her. But a contract was a contract, and he had work to do.

~

SARA WATCHED THROUGH HER RIFLE SCOPE AS THE MAN FROM THE pickup truck ran toward Delilah to check on her. After examining his victim and finding her unconscious, he went back to his truck and drove off. That action perplexed Sara until she saw the truck stop several hundred feet away, along the top of the ridge where there was less sand, and the trail's surface turned to rock. When the man left his pickup a second time he reached into the truck's bed and grabbed a push broom. After running back to the other end of the ridge where the hard-packed earth began turning into a sandy surface, he laid the broom down. He then retrieved Delilah's scooter, placed it upright, and rode it back to where he'd dropped the broom.

Sara was puzzled by his actions, but after he put that broom to work obliterating the tire tracks and footprints he'd made, she understood what he planned to do. Next, he would straddle the scooter, ride it over to the edge of the ridge near Delilah, and send it over. No doubt, Delilah would soon follow the scooter's path. With the only marks in the sand having been made by the scooter, Delilah's death would be ruled an accident, and no one would be the wiser. As her killer walked back to his truck, the broom could be used again to wipe out his shoe prints.

When the man sat on the scooter, Sara raised the rifle to her shoulder and took aim. She'd been shooting for distance with a rifle for years and had received training by the best—Tanner. She was a good shot at a stationary target, now Sara's skill would be used on a moving one during a life and death situation.

Her first shot struck Garcia on the outer portion of his left shoulder. She had been aiming for his head. Still, the slug took a chunk out of the man and sent him falling off the scooter.

Garcia's eyes were closed tight against the pain but when he opened them and looked around his eyes were wild with fear. He thought of himself as a predator, and now he had become prey to an unseen assailant.

He abandoned the scooter and lumbered toward his truck with blood leaking from the wound in his shoulder and turning his white shirt red. Sara's second shot missed by a hair and blew out the side window on the truck. The pickup's engine had been left running, so Garcia had it moving right away.

Sara fired again. The round passed through the truck's rear window and struck Delilah's would-be killer in his other shoulder. On the way there it had removed a chunk of his right ear.

The pickup lurched toward the precipice and Sara saw Garcia make a desperate attempt to right the front wheels. His effort came too late, and the truck drove off the edge, giving Garcia the fate he had envisioned for Delilah as he fell over forty feet. The sound of the truck's impact was loud, but there was no rising smoke or blaze following it, as there often was in the movies. The truck came to rest at the bottom of the sheer drop; its lone occupant lying dead.

Sara had taken a dozen steps in the direction where Delilah lay before catching herself and coming to a halt. There was no time to check on the girl's condition or to offer aid. Tanner needed her to fulfill her part of his plan, or the target might get away.

After gazing at Delilah through the rifle scope once more and assuring herself that Delilah was breathing, Sara began running in the other direction, toward her vehicle. She had to get to the place she needed to be that was miles away, and she had to do so soon. She had saved Delilah's life, and if the girl was injured, she would have to wait to receive aid. Tanner needed her, and she wasn't about to let him down.

∽

WHEN THREE O'CLOCK CAME, THE PHONE TANNER HAD PROVIDED rang and was answered by Kirk, who had been waiting inside his limousine with Aroke and a driver. They were parked halfway between the estate and Juarez.

Kirk spoke in an angry tone. "I want my stamps; tell me where to meet you."

Tanner, again using a southern accent, described a location that was a three-hour drive away from the estate, then told Kirk that he had only three hours to get there.

"You said I would have until midnight; I'll need more time."

"You won't get it. If I give you more time, you'll try to get there early and set up a trap. This way, we know you'll only have time to make the trip."

"But I'm not at the estate. It will take me longer to get there."

"Enough talk. Bring the money. This is your last chance. And oh yeah, there's one more thing, Harper."

"Yes?"

"We took photos of the paperwork you had in the safe. It was written in a language I don't know but I showed it to an expert. He said that it looked like some sort of an encoded ledger. Was he right?"

Kirk's face had paled a shade when Tanner mentioned having copies of the paperwork. They were an encrypted record, and one that detailed his drug business and the human trafficking he and Niko had been doing in their country. They had grabbed people off the street and sold them as either sex slaves or unwilling organ donors. Some of the organ donors had been hunted by Niko for sport prior to their lungs or kidney's being removed. Niko reasoned that they were going to be dead soon anyway, so why not have a little fun with them beforehand. Even in his absence from the country, those loyal to Kirk were shipping off prisoners of war to be used as organ donors, and women were still being rounded up for sex slaves. If the truth came out, he and Niko would be labeled as monsters.

"Are you still there?" Tanner asked.

"I'm here. How much do you want for the papers?"

"Nothing. We'll call it a bonus. But if you try anything, we'll make sure those papers wind up on the internet. Once they're on there, someone will figure out what they are. You have two hours and fifty-eight minutes left. I'd hurry if I was you."

The line went dead, and Kirk ordered the limo driver to head to the location he'd been given. "Drive fast. We've a deadline to beat."

~

MILES AWAY, TANNER CALLED HENRY. "IF KIRK DOESN'T REACT the way I expect, this whole plan is worthless."

"It will work. Like you've said all along, there's no way he would be willing to pay to get his stamps back. With a three-hour deadline, and with no money available, all he has left is to try to outsmart you again."

"We'll find out one way or the other. Get into position, then call and check on Sara. Her part in this is key."

"Will do," Henry said.

Tanner put his phone away, then looked at his watch. "C'mon, Kirk. Be predictable. Show us how clever you are."

~

Inside the limousine, Kirk was wearing a wide grin. He had thought of a way to get the upper hand. After telling the driver to change direction and head for the airfield where he kept his plane, he explained his plan to Aroke.

"There's an airport a short drive away from the location the thief named. We'll fly there, then rent a vehicle. That will put us in the area early and we'll be able to ambush them." Kirk took out his phone and called the security company he used to guard his plane. He explained to them that he would be using it shortly and asked for the phone number of the guard on duty. He was given the number and dialed the guard.

"This is Mr. Harper. I'll be at the airfield soon."

Kirk was asked to verify his identity by giving a code word. He did so, and the guard said he would be expecting him. His third call was to the office of the airfield where he kept his plane. When a man answered, Kirk told him who he was and that he wanted his plane prepared for flight.

"Move swiftly. I'll want to get in the air the moment I arrive. The guard knows that you'll be coming into the hangar."

With his calls made. Kirk turned his attention back to Aroke. "You'll be using your rifle. When we get there early, you'll be able to set up a sniper's nest. The man driving us to the airport can come along with us on the plane. That way, I won't be alone when the thieves show for the meeting."

Aroke took out a satellite phone. "I'll call the estate and have some of the guards join us, so you'll have more protection at the airfield."

"No. That would delay us. They'll waste time getting organized and gathering weapons. What's important is that we get to the rendezvous spot first."

"At least let a few of the guards meet us at the airfield. It shouldn't delay us more than ten minutes."

"Forget them, Aroke. I'm in a bulletproof limo and I'll soon be in the sky. If we hurry, we'll beat the deadline by an hour or more."

∼

Kirk was pounding a fist against his thigh in irritation when they drove up to the gate at the airfield. The trip had taken longer than usual because a pair of trucks had been hogging both lanes of the road. It was a delay of no more than a few minutes, but given the stakes and the ticking clock, each passing moment had been felt keenly by Kirk.

When he was through the airfield's gate and close enough to see that his plane was out of its hangar and running, he felt calmer and relaxed.

Aroke was the opposite and had tensed up. The airfield was an open area and there were dozens of places where an assassin could hide with a rifle to snipe at Kirk. From the time he left the limousine until the plane was in the air, Kirk would be in danger.

There was a man in coveralls and a cap completing the preflight inspection on the plane. Kirk called to him in Spanish as he left the limo. When the man didn't respond, Kirk spoke louder to be heard over the sound of the plane's engine.

"Is she ready to go!"

The man turned and was holding a silenced gun in his right hand. He was Tanner. "The plane is ready to go, and so are you."

Kirk made an incoherent sound as he took in Tanner's intense eyes, then he flinched as Tanner fired toward him. The round wasn't meant for Kirk, Tanner had been firing at Aroke.

His shot caught Aroke in the right hip and spun him around, making him collapse to one knee. The rifle Aroke held left his grip and skittered away.

Tanner's next shot found the man who'd driven the limo. He was only there because Tanner wanted to give Kirk the option of using Aroke to set up an ambush. With the third man along, Kirk wouldn't look odd meeting the "thieves" while alone. That was why he'd allowed Kirk to bring an extra man. It had the added benefit of making him feel more confident, and more likely to risk himself the way he had.

The limo driver had been removing a gun from a shoulder holster when Tanner shot him. The bullet struck him between the eyes and the guy stumbled into Kirk and knocked him off-balance. Kirk had a gun but decided not to go for it. Instead, he raised his hands, forced a smile, and spoke in English.

"You're Tanner, aren't you?"

"That's right."

"I'll pay you double what you're getting if you let me live."

"The stamp collection was payment enough."

Kirk's eyes widened and his mouth hung open. "That was you?"

"That was me. Goodbye, Hyena. I'm off to kill Niko next."

Kirk shouted the word, "No!" as Tanner fired. The first round entered his open mouth and exited out the back of his head. After Kirk's body was settled on the ground, Tanner placed one in his heart.

Lying a few feet away, Aroke was weeping. His eyes had already been tearing because of the intense pain in his hip but now the tears were spawned by an ache in his heart. In some ways, Kirk had been like a brother to him. Now the man was dead because he had failed to protect him.

Tanner walked over to Aroke and stared at him. After kicking the sniper rifle out of reach, he checked Aroke for other weapons and found only a knife, along with a satellite phone. After taking the weapons from the bodies of Kirk and the chauffeur, Tanner turned his back on Aroke and headed for the plane. His destination was the bunker. By air, he could be there in minutes.

∼

WEEKS EARLIER

AFTER RETURNING HOME FROM HIS FIRST TRIP TO JUAREZ TO check out the targets, Tanner had been torn about which Hyena brother to kill. They were both tough contracts and each offered a challenge. When he thought of going after Kirk at the estate, Tanner knew he would regret not having the opportunity to triumph over the bunker. And when he considered going after Niko in the bunker instead, he felt a sense of disappointment that had the tint of failure in it. The thought of handing off either contract to another assassin or a team of killers seemed wrong. He was a Tanner, and reputably the greatest assassin who'd ever lived. Shouldn't he be able to do the impossible?

Then he asked himself, If I had to, how would I go about killing both brothers within minutes of each other, although they were thirty miles apart? Once he put his mind to it, Tanner came up with a plan. While it would require daring and cunning as did most tough contracts, it also relied on human nature and would be a huge gamble.

Niko had many ways to leave that bunker, and he would do so before Tanner could fly to the area after killing his brother. Twenty men might not be able to locate him out in the vast desert, much less a lone man. The best way to kill Niko was to find a way into that bunker before he had a chance to escape. If Niko made it out and went into hiding, he might eventually make it back to Almalia and become its dictator again.

More importantly to Tanner, it will have meant that he failed to fulfill a contract that had a deadline attached. It would be the first failure any Tanner had ever suffered.

After spending an hour wondering if he was giving in to his ego by refusing to hand over one of the other contracts, Tanner decided that he wasn't, at least, satisfying his ego wasn't his main motivation. What drove him was his need to excel at his chosen profession. The challenge of killing two men who were thirty miles apart within a matter of minutes was a unique test of his skills. He'd spent his life wanting to be the best assassin in the world. By killing both brothers, one protected by fifty men, and the other secure in an underground bunker, Tanner would know that he had reached his goal.

When he contacted Thomas Lawson and stated that he wanted both contracts, he expected the man to protest and reiterate the price of failure. And while Lawson did express surprise at his decision to take on what seemed an incredible task, he didn't object.

"If you say you can do it, I believe you, although I'll be damned if I know how it can happen."

"I have a plan."

"Let me know when it's done or if you need assistance beforehand."

"Thomas."

"Yes?"

"Thanks for having faith in me."

"You're known for doing the impossible, Tanner. I would never doubt you when you tell me you can do something."

When the call ended, Tanner had sat at his desk inside his office at the ranch and went about refining the plan he had in mind.

~

WEEKS LATER, THE FIRST PART OF THAT PLAN WAS COMPLETED. Kirk Hyena was dead, and thanks to Kirk, Tanner had a plane ready that he could fly to reach the area where the bunker was located, to kill Niko. Better yet, by being at the airfield instead of the estate, he was several miles closer to Niko.

As he got the plane moving and was taxiing for takeoff, Tanner failed to see the armed guard leave the hangar with a rifle in his hands. As the plane's wheels left the ground, the guard took aim and fired.

26

CRASH AND BURN

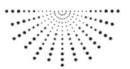

Aroke heard Kirk's satellite phone ring as Tanner had headed toward the plane. When the plane began moving, he grabbed the phone. It was Niko calling. The electronic bracelet he wore had alerted him that his brother's bracelet wasn't detecting a pulse. Niko had called Kirk to find out what was going on. Although the bracelet was flashing red and telling him that Kirk had been killed, Niko expected to hear his brother's voice.

Aroke answered Kirk's phone while grunting in pain, then he yelled into the phone. "The assassin Tanner killed Kirk. Run, Niko! Leave the bunker as fast as you can; Tanner is on his way there."

"What? Wait! Kirk is really dead?"

"Yes. And Tanner is headed your way in Kirk's plane. If he's doing that, it means he has a way to breach the bunker. You must—hold on!"

Aroke had spotted the man in the guard uniform come out of the hangar. Strips of duct tape clung to the cuffs of his pants and the sleeves of his uniform shirt. He must have been bound but had managed to get free. Even better, the man was holding a rifle with a long barrel.

The plane was off the ground and gaining altitude when the guard fired three times. Nothing happened at first, but then there was a loud popping noise that came from the plane, and smoke began streaming from it. The guard fired a final shot, but the plane was either out of range or the round had missed. Still, the guard's earlier shots had seemed to cause damage. Aroke watched the trail of smoke in the sky until he could no longer see the plane. He'd been so entranced by the scene before him that he momentarily forgot the agony in his hip and the phone in his hand. Then he became aware that Niko was shouting at him through the phone.

"What's going on there! Who's shooting?"

"The guard assigned to keep watch over the plane took shots at Tanner. He hit the plane and there's smoke coming out of it."

"Did it crash?"

"No, and now it's out of sight. But Tanner is still headed your way. Leave the bunker and contact me when you're safe."

"I'm safe here. I don't see any way that Tanner could breach the bunker's defenses."

"He killed Scallato, and Scallato was known for making impossible assassinations. Tanner can do the same. Don't underestimate the man; everyone who has is dead... including Kirk."

"I don't like running away from anyone."

"I know. And Tanner isn't just anyone. Run, Niko. Get away while you still can."

There was a moment of silence, then Niko spoke. "I'll leave, but I swear I'm going to kill Tanner someday for what he did to Kirk."

"I'll be at your side when that day comes."

The call ended, and Aroke collapsed onto his back, as the agony in his hip and his heart overwhelmed him.

∼

HYENAS

TANNER WAS STILL HEADED TOWARD THE BUNKER. HE'D HEARD the shots being fired at him but never felt their impact. When he turned his head to look out the plane's rear window, he could see the trail of smoke he was leaving behind. He ignored it but kept an eye on the aircraft's gauges, as he sped toward the bunker at over a hundred and twenty-five miles an hour.

∽

NIKO CHOSE TO LEAVE THE BUNKER THROUGH ONE OF THE LONGER tunnels, because it would place him closer to Juarez. The narrow tunnel wasn't as extended as the ones you had to crawl through, but it was over a mile long and too small to contain a car. What it did have was a dirt bike that had been designed for use in the desert. Aroke had checked the bike out when he'd been staying at the bunker. It had a full tank and there was a gun in a holster lying beside it. Next to that was a backpack containing food, water, a cell phone, and spare ammo.

There was one camera that provided a view of the exit. Niko saw nothing but a blank landscape on the screen. After entering a four-digit code into a keypad on the wall beside the camera, Niko pressed a green button and a section of the tunnel wall lifted like a garage door, although it was half the size of one.

Niko held the gun in his hand and eased toward the opening. When he cleared the entrance, he confirmed that he was alone. The dirt bike started on the first try and he rode it out a few yards, then stopped. Although it would take time to do so, he used the bunker's master remote to close the tunnel door behind him. When it was down, Niko saw that it was a hunk of stone that had graffiti written on it. The people who'd left their marks on the stone had had no idea what they'd been writing on.

Before taking off, Niko searched the skies for the plane Tanner was in. He saw nothing and began riding toward the highway. After climbing over a hill, he spotted a mountain lion in the distance. Niko was tempted to chase the animal down by using the bike so he could kill it, just for the hell of it, and to take out his frustration on the beast. When he realized that using the gun might give away his location, he continued riding toward the highway and let the mountain lion live.

He had traveled a fair distance away from the bunker when he had to navigate around three large sand dunes. By doing so, he'd momentarily been facing the way he had come and spotted the plane.

Actually, it wasn't the plane that had caught his attention but the smoke trailing behind it. As it drew closer, Niko saw that it was losing altitude. When it was closer still, he saw that it was on fire. Tanner had made it to the bunker, but he was about to crash.

∼

TANNER WAS CONCENTRATING ON LANDING THE PLANE, BUT HE couldn't help taking glances at the flame and smoke outside the windows. When he was no more than two hundred feet off the ground, he aimed the plane toward an area that was flatter than the land around it. To reach that valley, he had to clear a line of hills. There were more hills on the other side of that field. After landing, he would need to bring the airplane to a halt before he slammed into that second line of hills.

Heat from the fire was warming up the cockpit, but Tanner ignored it; if he wasn't careful, he could crash the plane. He cleared the hills but then the aircraft shuddered as something made a hissing noise, and Tanner braced for a hard landing.

∼

NIKO HAD BROUGHT THE DIRT BIKE TO A HALT SO HE COULD WATCH the plane. Knowing the area, he could see that Tanner was attempting to land the craft in a small valley that was east of the bunker. One of the many tunnels had an exit there. Maybe Tanner had plans to enter the bunker that way.

The assassin managed to clear the hills on the far side of the valley, but the plane was ablaze and giving off thick smoke. When the aircraft disappeared from his view, Niko cocked his head and listened. He was rewarded by the sound he'd been hoping to hear, that of an explosion. Although miles away, the sound carried well in the silence of the desert.

Niko thrust a fist over his head and made a sound of joy. If not dead, Tanner was certainly injured from the crash.

Black smoke drifted toward the sky from the floor of the valley and was growing thicker. Niko headed the dirt bike in that direction. If Tanner had survived, he wouldn't be alive for long, and if dead, he would piss on his body.

∼

NIKO RODE THE BIKE UP THE SIDE OF AN EIGHTY-FOOT-HIGH HILL and saw the site of the crash. The plane looked as if it had broken in half on impact and fire was consuming the pieces.

Movement caught his eye, and through the smoke he saw a figure crawling away while on its hands and knees. It was a bloody figure, and one of its legs was being dragged behind it.

Tanner! Niko thought. Bloodlust, rage, and a desire for vengeance roiled within him and he left the dirt bike to scramble down the steep hill and race toward the man who'd killed his brother.

Niko slackened his speed as he passed the burning wreck. With his gun in his hand, he approached the slowly moving figure; he did so by following behind the streak of red it was leaving in its path.

"Tanner! You killed Kirk you son of a bitch, and now you're going to die."

The figure kept crawling, and the head didn't turn to look at him. Niko was about to shout Tanner's name again when a rifle round tore through his left knee. The shout became a scream of agony and Niko collapsed to the ground. A second shot blasted through his right arm and nearly severed it at the elbow.

Niko was staring up at the sky and breathing rapidly through an open mouth when two people approached him; one was a man and the other was a woman. The woman was beautiful, and she stayed back several yards. The man was Tanner, and he moved in for the kill. Not the injured and bloody Tanner who had been crawling along in tattered, bloodstained clothes, but a healthy Tanner who didn't have a mark on him.

Niko gritted his teeth against a wave of pain, then managed to gasp out three words, "What the fuck?"

Tanner was a man of fewer words. He said, "Goodbye, Niko," and shot Niko Hyena in the head. Twenty-seven minutes after killing Kirk Hyena, Tanner fulfilled the contract on his brother. He couldn't have done it without Niko's help.

27
SETTING THE TRAP

Tanner had crafted the strategy to use Kirk Hyena's love of his stamp collection against him by luring him to the airfield without his small army of guards around him. Even if that succeeded as planned, there was still the difficulty of killing Kirk's brother to deal with.

Given the labyrinth of tunnels at the bunker, and its considerable defenses, Tanner concluded it would be easier to lure Niko to him than it would be to find a way inside the bunker. Once he began looking at the problem of killing Niko in that light, he had little trouble coming up with a plan.

Thanks to the technology in the bracelets the Hyena brothers wore, Niko would be aware that Kirk had died. He'd be aware, but would he be willing to believe it without verifying it? That didn't seem likely. It was always possible the bracelets could malfunction, and a call to Kirk would certainly be made. If dead, Kirk couldn't answer a call, but someone could. That someone had been Aroke, who Tanner had left alive intentionally.

Not only could Aroke confirm Kirk's death, but he also made for a reliable and trusted witness, reliable, but deceived. The "guard" who had fired on the plane with a rifle had been Henry. The real guard had been drugged and hidden from view minutes earlier. Between the time he'd been rendered unconscious and Kirk's arrival at the airfield, Tanner and Henry had attached custom-made components onto the plane. One of those components could be turned on to emit smoke and another one created flame. The third one, the one that made the hissing sound when the plane's altitude dropped below a hundred feet, was filled with fire retardant. That was a precaution to douse a blaze on any part of the plane that might have caught fire for real.

Tanner used the smoke and fire to attract Niko's attention, and to make him believe the plane was likely to have a rough landing. And although Tanner had touched down hard in the small valley and damaged a wheel on the plane, he hadn't crashed. The sound Niko had heard had been made by Sara. She had ignited a canister filled with explosives. Earlier, with the use of a truck, she had driven into the valley and unloaded the vehicle's cargo. Inside the truck had been a lightweight replica of the exterior of Kirk's plane. The reproduction was in two pieces, and they appeared as if they had been mangled on impact. When she saw Tanner land the real airplane, she ignited the explosives and set fire to the craft's replica.

Afterward, Sara helped Tanner use a sand-colored tarp to cover up the plane he had landed in. The camouflage wasn't perfect, but it didn't need to be. Anyone cresting a hill and looking down inside the valley would have their gaze captured by what appeared to be a crashed airplane on fire.

It had certainly seized Niko's attention, and like a moth to a flame he walked into Tanner's trap. Had he kept running like he was supposed to, Niko would have survived. Tanner had bet on him not being able to pass on a chance to kill him, especially when Niko had reason to believe he was injured and far from his lethal best.

The battered and bloody figure Niko had taken to be Tanner was a creation of Duke's daughter, Lisa. Lisa had designed the mechanical dummy so that it would move along the ground at a snail's pace. Sara had placed it next to the bogus plane and opened the valve on it where fake blood was stored, so it would leave a trail in its wake.

It all would have been an enormous waste of time, effort, and expense if Niko had ignored it. But no, a man like Niko couldn't resist the chance to seek revenge. And if Tanner had died in the crash, he would have reveled in seeing his corpse. Tanner was certain the one thing he wouldn't do was ride away to wonder at his fate.

∽

THEY REACHED THE TRUCK SARA HAD USED TO TRANSPORT THE fake plane and Tanner asked her to drive. He was sending off a text to Lawson telling him that the contracts had been fulfilled.

Three figures appeared at the top of a hill some distance away. Given their silhouettes, they looked like they were hikers wearing backpacks. The sounds and the smoke had drawn them in to investigate.

"Let's get out of here before more people show up," Tanner said. As Sara drove, he studied the remote-control device he'd taken off Niko's body. It was a safe bet that it had something to do with the bunker. While he was tempted to use it to gain entry to the underground lair and explore it, he didn't think it wise. If he pressed the wrong button or made some other mistake there was a chance that safeguards inside the bunker would activate. He'd ship the device off to Thomas Lawson and let him send people to the bunker to figure it out. His work was done.

"Where is Henry?" Sara asked.

"Henry will meet us back at the hotel."

"I need to make a stop first," Sara said, then she explained to Tanner what had happened to Delilah earlier.

"She's lucky you were there to watch over her."

"I need to know if she's all right."

They drove for twelve minutes and reached the spot where

Sara had last seen Delilah. The girl was gone along with her scooter. A look over the side of the cliff revealed the mangled pickup truck. There was a line of drying blood running from it.

"She must have woken up and driven off," Sara said.

"That means she's all right."

"I have a favor to ask of you."

"What is it?"

When Sara explained, Tanner nodded. "That sounds like a good idea."

They left the desert and headed toward their hotel. Two difficult contracts were fulfilled, and at the hands of one man— A Tanner.

28

A PARTING GIFT

DELILAH HAD SUFFERED THROUGH THE WORST DAYS OF HER LIFE. She had awoken lying on the ground with a headache and realized that she had crashed her scooter. She had thought it was her own fault until she remembered getting a glimpse of a pickup truck before being knocked out. Having some medical knowledge, Delilah realized she might have suffered a concussion, although she wasn't dizzy. After arriving late to school to pick up her brother, she returned home to find a neighbor waiting for her. The neighbor was a kindly old woman who would keep an eye on Tomás for her occasionally. Delilah could tell by the woman's grim expression that something bad had happened. And that was how she found out her mother had died.

Delilah's mother had roused herself from bed only to venture out for more liquor. To buy it, she had stolen money from the piggy bank in Tomás room. While at the store, she suffered a fatal heart attack. Delilah cried at the loss of her mother although in some ways she had lost the woman to addiction years earlier. The next day, she learned of Niko's death and wept more. Along with the grieving came worry, as she wondered what the future would bring.

∽

Delilah walked out of her apartment building and straddled her scooter; she was headed to the market to buy groceries. She was about to put her helmet on when she noticed the man walking toward her. He was white, handsome, in his forties, and had on glasses. Despite the suit he wore, Delilah could tell the man was in shape.

It was Tanner; he smiled at her.

"Delilah Ortiz."

"Yes?"

"My name is Myers. I understand you were close to Niko Hyena. I'm sorry for your loss."

"You knew Niko?"

"We met once. Miss Ortiz, I have something Niko would have wanted you to have."

Tanner opened the briefcase, reached inside, and brought out a large white envelope. He handed it to Delilah.

"Mr. Hyena arranged for you to have that should anything happen to him. He wanted to make sure you were provided for."

Delilah opened the heavy envelope and her eyes looked as if they might pop out of her head.

"This is so much money. Niko left this for me?"

"It's twenty-five thousand in American dollars and more than half a million pesos. You'll also find instructions advising you on the best way to secure it and avoid paying taxes. It's enough money to start a new life for you and your brother."

Delilah's mouth was hanging open in shock. "I can keep this? It's all mine?"

"Yes. Use it wisely. Maybe go back to school."

Delilah was nodding. "Are you a lawyer?"

"I'm what you might call a problem solver; I hope I've helped to solve yours. Goodbye."

Tanner walked away and got behind the wheel of his vehicle. Sara was in the passenger seat.

"Thank you for doing that. I think that girl deserves a new start."

"And what better way to do it than with the money I took from Kirk Hyena's safe. I'm sure he was the one who tried to have her killed."

"Delilah got the money, and you gave away the watches, but what about Kirk Hyena's stamps?"

"I'll place them in the safe back at home. I'm sure they'll come in useful someday."

"I'm glad we're leaving tomorrow; I miss the children."

"So do I, but we've one more night in Juarez. What would you like to do?"

When she said nothing, Tanner turned and looked at Sara. The lascivious smile she wore told him what she was thinking. They would be spending the night in the bedroom of their hotel suite; that didn't mean they would be getting much sleep.

Tanner drove a little faster as he headed toward the hotel, and Kirk and Niko Hyena were no more than a memory.

TANNER RETURNS!

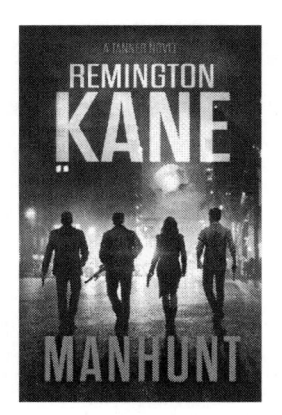

MANHUNT - TANNER 46 - AVAILABLE FOR PRE-ORDER - ON SALE APRIL 30th.

AFTERWORD

Thank you,

REMINGTON KANE

JOIN MY INNER CIRCLE

You'll receive FREE books, such as,

SLAY BELLS – A TANNER NOVEL – BOOK 0

TAKEN! ALPHABET SERIES – 26 ORIGINAL TAKEN! TALES

BLUE STEELE - KARMA

Also – Exclusive short stories featuring TANNER, along with other books.

TO BECOME AN INNER CIRCLE MEMBER, GO TO:
http://remingtonkane.com/mailing-list/

ALSO BY REMINGTON KANE

The TANNER Series in order

INEVITABLE I - A Tanner Novel - Book 1
KILL IN PLAIN SIGHT - A Tanner Novel - Book 2
MAKING A KILLING ON WALL STREET - A Tanner Novel - Book 3
THE FIRST ONE TO DIE LOSES - A Tanner Novel - Book 4
THE LIFE & DEATH OF CODY PARKER - A Tanner Novel - Book 5
WAR - A Tanner Novel- A Tanner Novel - Book 6
SUICIDE OR DEATH - A Tanner Novel - Book 7
TWO FOR THE KILL - A Tanner Novel - Book 8
BALLET OF DEATH - A Tanner Novel - Book 9
MORE DANGEROUS THAN MAN - A Tanner Novel - Book 10
TANNER TIMES TWO - A Tanner Novel - Book 11
OCCUPATION: DEATH - A Tanner Novel - Book 12
HELL FOR HIRE - A Tanner Novel - Book 13
A HOME TO DIE FOR - A Tanner Novel - Book 14
FIRE WITH FIRE - A Tanner Novel - Book 15
TO KILL A KILLER - A Tanner Novel - Book 16
WHITE HELL – A Tanner Novel - Book 17
MANHATTAN HIT MAN – A Tanner Novel - Book 18
ONE HUNDRED YEARS OF TANNER – A Tanner Novel - Book 19
REVELATIONS - A Tanner Novel - Book 20
THE SPY GAME - A Tanner Novel - Book 21
A VICTIM OF CIRCUMSTANCE - A Tanner Novel - Book 22
A MAN OF RESPECT - A Tanner Novel - Book 23
THE MAN, THE MYTH - A Tanner Novel - Book 24

ALL-OUT WAR - A Tanner Novel - Book 25
THE REAL DEAL - A Tanner Novel - Book 26
WAR ZONE - A Tanner Novel - Book 27
ULTIMATE ASSASSIN - A Tanner Novel - Book 28
KNIGHT TIME - A Tanner Novel - Book 29
PROTECTOR - A Tanner Novel - Book 30
BULLETS BEFORE BREAKFAST - A Tanner Novel - Book 31
VENGEANCE - A Tanner Novel - Book 32
TARGET: TANNER - A Tanner Novel - Book 33
BLACK SHEEP - A Tanner Novel - Book 34
FLESH AND BLOOD - A Tanner Novel - Book 35
NEVER SEE IT COMING - A Tanner Novel - Book 36
MISSING - A Tanner Novel - Book 37
CONTENDER - A Tanner Novel - Book 38
TO SERVE AND PROTECT - A Tanner Novel - Book 39
STALKING HORSE - A Tanner Novel - Book 40
THE EVIL OF TWO LESSERS - A Tanner Novel - Book 41
SINS OF THE FATHER AND MOTHER - A Tanner Novel - Book 42
SOULLESS - A Tanner Novel - Book 43
LIT FUSE - A Tanner Novel - Book 44
HYENAS - A Tanner Novel - Book 45
MANHUNT - A Tanner Novel - Book 46

The Young Guns Series in order

YOUNG GUNS
YOUNG GUNS 2 - SMOKE & MIRRORS
YOUNG GUNS 3 - BEYOND LIMITS
YOUNG GUNS 4 - RYKER'S RAIDERS
YOUNG GUNS 5 - ULTIMATE TRAINING
YOUNG GUNS 6 - CONTRACT TO KILL

YOUNG GUNS 7 - FIRST LOVE
YOUNG GUNS 8 - THE END OF THE BEGINNING

A Tanner Series in order

TANNER: YEAR ONE
TANNER: YEAR TWO
TANNER: YEAR THREE
TANNER: YEAR FOUR
TANNER: YEAR FIVE

The TAKEN! Series in order

TAKEN! - LOVE CONQUERS ALL - Book 1
TAKEN! - SECRETS & LIES - Book 2
TAKEN! - STALKER - Book 3
TAKEN! - BREAKOUT! - Book 4
TAKEN! - THE THIRTY-NINE - Book 5
TAKEN! - KIDNAPPING THE DEVIL - Book 6
TAKEN! - HIT SQUAD - Book 7
TAKEN! - MASQUERADE - Book 8
TAKEN! - SERIOUS BUSINESS - Book 9
TAKEN! - THE COUPLE THAT SLAYS TOGETHER - Book 10
TAKEN! - PUT ASUNDER - Book 11
TAKEN! - LIKE BOND, ONLY BETTER - Book 12
TAKEN! - MEDIEVAL - Book 13
TAKEN! - RISEN! - Book 14
TAKEN! - VACATION - Book 15
TAKEN! - MICHAEL - Book 16
TAKEN! - BEDEVILED - Book 17
TAKEN! - INTENTIONAL ACTS OF VIOLENCE - Book 18

TAKEN! - THE KING OF KILLERS – Book 19
TAKEN! - NO MORE MR. NICE GUY - Book 20 & the Series Finale

The MR. WHITE Series

PAST IMPERFECT - MR. WHITE - Book 1
HUNTED - MR. WHITE - Book 2

The BLUE STEELE Series in order

BLUE STEELE - BOUNTY HUNTER- Book 1
BLUE STEELE - BROKEN- Book 2
BLUE STEELE - VENGEANCE- Book 3
BLUE STEELE - THAT WHICH DOESN'T KILL ME- Book 4
BLUE STEELE - ON THE HUNT- Book 5
BLUE STEELE - PAST SINS - Book 6
BLUE STEELE - DADDY'S GIRL - Book 7 & the Series Finale

The CALIBER DETECTIVE AGENCY Series in order

CALIBER DETECTIVE AGENCY - GENERATIONS- Book 1
CALIBER DETECTIVE AGENCY - TEMPTATION- Book 2
CALIBER DETECTIVE AGENCY - A RANSOM PAID IN BLOOD- Book 3
CALIBER DETECTIVE AGENCY - MISSING- Book 4
CALIBER DETECTIVE AGENCY - DECEPTION- Book 5
CALIBER DETECTIVE AGENCY - CRUCIBLE- Book 6
CALIBER DETECTIVE AGENCY – LEGENDARY – Book 7
CALIBER DETECTIVE AGENCY – WE ARE GATHERED HERE TODAY - Book 8
CALIBER DETECTIVE AGENCY - MEANS, MOTIVE, and OPPORTUNITY - Book 9 & the Series Finale

THE TAKEN!/TANNER Series in order

THE CONTRACT: KILL JESSICA WHITE - Taken!/Tanner - Book 1
UNFINISHED BUSINESS – Taken!/Tanner – Book 2
THE ABDUCTION OF THOMAS LAWSON - Taken!/Tanner – Book 3
PREDATOR - Taken!/Tanner - Book 4

DETECTIVE PIERCE Series in order

MONSTERS - A Detective Pierce Novel - Book 1
DEMONS - A Detective Pierce Novel - Book 2
ANGELS - A Detective Pierce Novel - Book 3

THE OCEAN BEACH ISLAND Series in order

THE MANY AND THE ONE - Book 1
SINS & SECOND CHANES - Book 2
DRY ADULTERY, WET AMBITION - Book 3
OF TONGUE AND PEN - Book 4
ALL GOOD THINGS… - Book 5
LITTLE WHITE SINS - Book 6
THE LIGHT OF DARKNESS - Book 7
STERN ISLAND - Book 8 & the Series Finale

THE REVENGE Series in order

JOHNNY REVENGE - The Revenge Series - Book 1
THE APPOINTMENT KILLER - The Revenge Series - Book 2
AN I FOR AN I - The Revenge Series - Book 3

ALSO

THE EFFECT: Reality is changing!
THE FIX-IT MAN: A Tale of True Love and Revenge

DOUBLE OR NOTHING

PARKER & KNIGHT

REDEMPTION: Someone's taken her

DESOLATION LAKE

TIME TRAVEL TALES & OTHER SHORT STORIES

HYENAS
Copyright © REMINGTON KANE, 2021
YEAR ZERO PUBLISHING, LLC

This book is a work of fiction. Names, characters, places and incidents either are products of the author's imagination or are used fictitiously.

Any resemblance to actual events or locales or persons, living or dead, is entirely coincidental.

All rights reserved. Except as permitted under the U.S. Copyright Act of 1976, no part of this publication may be reproduced, distributed or transmitted in any form or by any means, or stored in a database or retrieval system, without the prior written permission of the publisher.

❦ Created with Vellum

Made in the USA
Middletown, DE
15 February 2025